The Ghosts of Spirit Town
Spirit Town Cozy Mystery Book 3
Sarah Lewin © 2025

Secrets Ghosts and Whispers
Book #2 Spirit Town Cosy Mystery

First edition October 2024
ISBN 978-0-6458504-8-2 (ebook)
ISBN 978-1-7637430-2-1 (Paperback)
www.sarahlewin.com[1]

---

1. http://www.sarahlewin.com

Chapter One

I breathed in the scent of geraniums and roses, running my fingers along the plants I helped my grandma plant over twenty years ago. If I closed my eyes, I could imagine she sat beside me, with my parents, on our front verandah, with the white picket railing, the blue and grey tones, amidst the fragrant flowers. "How did I not know my parents and my grandmother spent years ensuring the safety of the inhabitants of our town?" I stamped my feet on the wooden floorboards under my comfy fluffy purple slippers and crossed my arms. I knew I sounded like a petulant child.

My best friend, Seamus sat opposite me on one of the wicker chairs where we used to sit to do our homework, all those years ago. His thick wavy hair was still dark, not yet peppered with grey, despite us both being close to forty. His deep blue eyes laughed, but he said nothing. He simply passed the tub of peppermint chocolate chip ice cream to me. The silver spoon stood up in what was left of the icy dessert.

I eyed the spoon but made no move to take it from its icy sheath. "I can't figure out if they deliberately lied to me, or simply didn't tell me what was going on, thinking they were protecting me." I wished he'd speak, say anything to either confirm my thinking, or challenge me.

"You did make a point of renouncing anything to do with your abilities, in high school. You left town so quickly," Seamus shook his head, sadness in his eyes. "I know they always hoped you'd return. I'm sure they wanted to tell you, and would have told you, if they'd had the opportunity." He stopped speaking so abruptly, I knew there had to be more.

"What did you just remember? I won't be upset," I picked up the spoon, turning it over with my fingers. I wanted to taste the sweet ice cream, my favourite flavour, but something held me back. My stubbornness. How could I eat ice cream if I was still angry at my parents? *Seriously Beth!*

"I don't think you realise this, but your grandmother wanted to teach you the old ways. She wished to pass along the knowledge that had been passed to her. She started to. I remember you both loved spending time in the garden, she'd read to you, and you were always cooking together in the kitchen. Then there was her collection of herbs and crystals, or rocks as I used to call them. They scared me, but you'd spend hours in her room." Seamus cast his eyes down, studying the old wooden tabletop. His fingers rubbed the surface, concentrating on the worn timber. "Your parents forbade it, and Grandma respected their decision, though she didn't agree. Your dad talked to me about it, years later, wondering if they'd made the right decision. Your parents were beginning to regret not teaching you more about your abilities. They tried so hard to make sure you experienced a normal childhood. They asked me not to tell you about the conversation, they didn't want you to feel obligated to come home," Seamus looked at me, tears welling in his deep blue eyes.

I tasted the hot salty tears as they trickled down my cheeks. "I'm not angry, I'm pleased you stayed in contact with them, spent time with them, and that they could talk to you. I could kick myself for being so stubborn..."

"It's who you are Beth, and why we love you," his cheeks reddened. "I mean...you do know your parents, and grandma are proud of you. You returned home, you helped save our town's festival, you uncovered a corrupt council, nominated as mayor and fought for all our residents, against powerful forces. From heaven or the other side, or beyond the veil, whatever you call it, they are watching, and they are proud of you."

I wanted to say *I couldn't have done any of it without your help and support*. I wanted to reach over and grab his hand and hold on tight. I didn't, remembering that when I first returned, and we both felt the attraction from days of old, I shut it down. I'd explained that we both needed to focus on our businesses. I'd inherited the local newspaper office, and Seamus had a farm and couple of small businesses. We managed to stay best friends, solving several mysteries together. Over a year later, we were both on council, and now ghostly forces were determined to stop me. When I returned to bury my parents, I'd not planned on staying. That changed as unseen forces in this town where magical and non-magical folk lived side by side, left me no option but to make my life here.

The realisation hit me like a ton of bricks. I didn't want to do it all alone. Heat rose in my cheeks, knowing that my bestie had the uncanny knack of reading my mind. "I couldn't have done any of it by myself," I felt my face redden even more. "I couldn't have done it without you." My body tingled, as I reached for Seamus's hand. As our fingers touched, sparks flew, like fireflies lighting the sky. After a few seconds, we reluctantly untangled our hands. Words left unspoken, hanging between us.

"If you're not going to eat any ice cream, hand it over," Seamus grinned, lightening the mood. I saw it in his smiling eyes – hope. His hand curled around the spoon, to drag the tub towards himself. I knew, we both knew, we wanted to be more than friends. I'd been the one stalling, firstly by running away for twenty years, then citing the need to focus on our businesses. Now, I wasn't sure I'd made the right call.

I grabbed the spoon, and his hand. "You just hang on there, my turn first."

Seamus rolled his eyes. "You're always first, and you have the last word as well." He released his hold on the cutlery, drumming his fingers on the table as he waited his turn.

I savoured the sugary sweet, chocolatey, peppermint taste, as the cold confectionary sent shivers through my mouth. I'd have to think about work, plan my week, and figure out what to do about the sinister threat to our town, but I was enjoying this, the peace and quiet, the ice cream, and the company.

"What are your plans for the week?" Seamus asked innocently, "It's not like you to rest, even on a Sunday."

"Good question," I handed the tub of ice cream over. "Wait here, I'll grab my laptop." I rose from our haven, crossing to the front door, before Seamus could comment any further. Spark, my ginger kitten, uncurled himself from his cushion beside us, and followed me inside. I picked my laptop up off the kitchen table, where I'd been making notes earlier. I checked the kettles water level, turned it on, and made a couple of peppermint teas.

"To compliment the dessert," I slid the two mugs onto the table.

"Laptop?" Seamus raised his eyebrows.

"Hey presto!" I pulled the computer out from its hiding place under my arm, tucked into my oversized purple cardigan.

"You should audition for a position at *The Magic Shop*," my friend quipped. One of the newest shops in town, it sold a selection of tools for learning magic tricks, ironic for a town where a good proportion of the inhabitants inherited a range of magical abilities. I'd mixed feelings about the establishment, with its gimmicky magic sets in the front, and other darker magic tools hidden out the back.

I opened my laptop and brought up the word document I'd been working on earlier. "It's all on the list," I swung the screen around for Seamus to see.

He shimmied his chair closer to mine, and read my list – "Investigate magic shop, research Dean Collier, research Jacob, look into council members and connections to corporations, investigate family," he gently closed the laptop. "Your parents weren't perfect, but they loved you. They would have told you about their connection to the magical community when you came home, expressed an interest..."

"Except that I didn't. and they died, were killed, because of their role in that community. My grandma too, likely lost her life because of her heritage, our heritage." I'd never stop regretting my decision to run away from who I was, my magic, or for staying away for twenty years.

"You're in the unique position that you can communicate with your deceased relatives. Not all gifted folk have your level of ability, or that connection with generations past. Regret won't get you the answers you need," he stood and stretched. "We could sit here all afternoon and go back and forth over old ground, or we could do something to take our mind off it." He picked up his mug, drinking his tea in one swallow.

I finished my tea, took the spoon out of what remained of the ice cream and replaced its lid. "What were you thinking?"

"There's a family fun day at the showground. Hosted by the local churches to raise awareness of the challenges of the local homeless, and to raise funds for them." He checked his watch. "It runs until 3pm, so if we leave now, it should still be in full swing."

Seamus followed me inside, carrying the ice cream and mugs. I returned my laptop to the kitchen table and filled Spark's little saucer with milk. "We won't be too long Spark. I don't expect more ghostly visitors, so you curl up in your bed and we'll see you soon." My kitten purred, rubbing his body around my legs. With a last look up at me, he wandered over to the saucer, his tiny tongue lapping up the drink.

I swapped my purple cardigan for the black one draped over the kitchen chair, and kicked my slippers off, replacing them with black shoes. As mayor, I tried to always appear presentable in public. My jeans and black shirt were new enough I didn't need to change them. With his blue denim jeans and thick blue checked shirt Seamus always managed to look both respectable and approachable. Perfect attributes for a businessman, council member, and boyfriend.

Chapter Two

A black crow greeted us with a caw as we returned to the verandah. He stood perched on the white railing, staring at us. "I hope you'll do a good job protecting our house while we're gone," I told him. He repeated his caw, which I took to be his willingness to guard my home.

"Are we walking or driving?" I asked, heading towards Seamus vehicle, pre-empting his response.

"Driving, if you don't mind. We might stop in at the café afterwards or get sidetracked and need to drive somewhere." Seamus knew how much I loved to walk, but he made a persuasive argument. With the mysteries and secrets following us, we often ended up running unplanned errands.

"Plus, if we do call in to the café, it'll be dark and cold by the time we head home. Good call," I agreed with his suggestion, mainly to see the look of surprise on his face.

"Are you feeling okay?" he joked, unlocking his ute. I smiled, as I stepped up into the passenger seat of Seamus's big blue farm truck. It towered over my little green hatchback. The energy between us buzzed, the familiar emotions we'd experienced as teens returning the longer the amount of time we spent together.

The short drive was uneventful. "They put a lot of time and effort into the preparation," I commented, noting the blue and orange flags temporarily erected at the entrance to the showground, indicating the entrance to the event. More cars than I could count lined up in the makeshift parking lot. "It looks like a good turnout."

"Most of the locals will support community events. Like our annual festival, they love the opportunity to help out, dress up, and buy local goods. Who doesn't like a good sausage sizzle?" I could practically hear his stomach growling as he parked at the end of a row.

"You just love food. If I ate half as much as you, I'd have to go for a run every day and I'd still be the size of an elephant," I laughed.

"It's in the genes," he quipped. The Quinns were third, or maybe fourth generation local farmers. As we were both only children, we spent most of the weekends at my house, or the Quinn family farm. His parents were as fit, wiry and energetic as Seamus.

I turned to my friend, "I don't remember them as being as ravenous as you," I chuckled. "I did love their huge pasta meals and pizzas, hey maybe you're right after all." I jumped out of the ute, easily falling in step beside my friend as we passed through the gates, dropping a donation into the bright yellow bucket.

A couple of elves sat cross legged on the table next to the bucket. "Hey, thanks for coming and for your donation. Check out the stalls and there's still time to enter the three-legged race," the elf on the left, wearing emerald green pants and a red stripy top smiled at us.

"Thanks Barry," Seamus responded with a grin. Always in awe with his gift of being able to talk to everyone, I shouldn't have been surprised he knew the elves by name. "Great game the other night Brice," he added. The elf with the navy trousers and lime green shirt grinned, holding both thumbs up. Seamus turned to me, "Brice here doesn't say much, but he plays a mean game of bucketball."

I refrained from asking how to play the game, choosing instead to smile at the elves, as we continued towards the row of multi coloured flags indicating the individual stalls and food vendors. I counted at least thirty stalls, including gourmet foods, local produce and home-made goods. A three-piece band were playing music I recognised from my teen years. Couples and families made use of the plastic chairs dotted around, to eat and listen to the music. "This was organised by the churches?" I asked.

My friend nodded, as he waved to some of the residents, that I knew by face, though their names escaped me. "Uhuh, why do you ask?"

I watched the elves helping on the white elephant stall, and the fairies helping hand out fairy floss. "I'd never thought about how a church in Spirit Town might welcome the magical beings...isn't magic a contradiction to mainstream religion?"

"I suppose, normally, anywhere else. Here we embrace the magic around us. Like I said before, your parents were instrumental in making sure Spirit Town was a place that welcomes people with unusual abilities. They worked with Agnes and the council...I know they hoped you'd feel comfortable enough to return." His lip trembled as his eyes filled with sadness. "I don't mean to keep telling you that, but it's important, especially now. You know that your grandmother and parents were leaders in the council that expelled people for using their skills in a way that harmed others, and that they were killed because of that. You'll continue to be a target, but I'm convinced your family will keep providing clues from beyond the veil, to help you beat whatever happens." He grabbed my hand, "Before we eat, are you game for the three-legged race?"

"Why not," I agreed letting him lead me to the starting line. Seamus was right. Since I'd returned, I'd had altercations with a corrupt mayor, a corporation wanting to knock down a row of shops my parents owned, and I inherited a newspaper office. When I stepped up as mayor, I'd been falsely accused of being involved in another corrupt corporation and targeted by a coven made up of former residents that my family banished years before. "Do you agree with the concept of banishing people who use their magic for the wrong reasons? You know so many people in town, have you noticed any changes since my parents died? I know the community members, like Agnes took on some leadership..."

"Geez Beth, we're supposed to be having fun," Seamus grinned, only pretending to be exasperated. "I get your mind never stops, but if I promise to talk about this over dinner, can we just pretend we're not in the middle of a mystery?"

I laughed, "Sure."

A petit elderly lady with short curly hair, wearing a light pink dress handed Seamus a long piece of stretchy material. "Good to see you young Quinn," she smiled, "Have you heard from your parents? They must be having so much fun, cruising around the world."

Seamus knelt, tying his left leg to my right. "Thanks Pearl. Yes, they're having a blast, and sending me lots of photos. I'll mention you asked after them next time we talk." His hand brushed my leg, causing tingles up my spine, even through the fabric of my jeans.

"It's good to see you out and about Beth," Pearl, a friend of my grandma's, had known me all my life.

I gave her a quick hug, careful not to fall over, with the restraint on my leg. "I'm always out these days, as mayor," I smiled at her, "It's nice to come out, have fun, be part of the community." My energy buzzed, I felt lighter than normal. Being in public didn't come easily to me, but the older I got, I found it worried me less. Was I finally growing up?

"Seamus, Beth! I'm so glad you made it." I recognised Lara's voice instantly. We became friends when we worked together to solve the mystery of the town gates, the cattle and other bizarre events that threatened to ruin our towns annual festival. A relative newcomer to town, she owned and managed the local health food store. Her honey blonde hair tied in a pigtail, her right leg tied to Jon's left leg, she smiled as we drew nearer. Our local policeman, Jon also new to town, had been invaluable in solving the mysteries of Spirit Town. Thrown into the middle of the chaos, successfully navigating the unusual nuances of our town in his first week on the job.

"Lara, Jon!" I smiled, genuinely happy to see them both. "I'm pleased I let Seamus drag me along." The electricity zooming through my body I'd not felt for a while. That carefree energy, a result of spending time with friends, having fun. Even I knew I took life far too seriously. Seamus squeezed my hand. He often read my mind, less often, I tuned into his. At this moment I knew he felt the same.

"I wasn't sure if you'd make it, after the last couple of weeks," Jon turned, almost falling on top of Lara. She held out her arm to steady him.

After meeting Jacob, a male cousin I didn't know existed, I learnt that my parents and grandmother, who I adored, had kept secrets from me. Not on purpose, which was much worse. My parents asked Grandma not to talk to me about our magic skills. As I grew older, I wasn't interested in my skills, leaving town because of them. If I'd bothered to return home, my parent could have told me, and who knows, maybe they'd still be alive. Then there was Dean, someone who decided to spend his time taunting me, telling lies about me and my ethics. Generally making my life challenging.

A teen dressed in a bright green vest held up an orange flag. "On your marks, get set, go!" He blew a little silver whistle, attached to a string around his neck. Seamus and I joined Lara and Jon and the three other couples, as we half tumbled, half galloped towards the finishing line ten metres away from where we stood. A tall man with grey hair, partnered with a much shorter grey-haired woman fell first – laughing as they tried to get up. A younger couple swerved too far left to miss the oldies, falling themselves, dissolving into laughter.

I didn't know whether we should stop and help or keep going. Lara must have been thinking the same, as we both hesitated just long enough for the other couple still on their feet to jump over the pink stripe of paint indicating the finish. "That's why we'll win every time Madam Mayor," sneered the man in black lycra leggings. His equally long-legged female companion nodded, her ponytail swishing, emphasizing their point of view.

While I tried to find the words, Seamus responded, "Caring beats competition every time." He turned away from the winners, holding out his hand and easing the older gentleman to his feet. I assisted the woman tied to his leg, while Jon untied the material from their legs.

A few seconds later, I glanced back to the finish line, hoping for a closer look at the winning team. They'd vanished. "Does anyone know who the winners are?" I asked.

Chapter Three

Seamus and I joined Lara and Jon, as we wandered through the food stalls. "It's weird that not even you knew who they were," I pointed out to Seamus.

"Too hungry to think," he held the back of his hand up to his forehead dramatically. "I'm sure a dagwood dog or some twisty potatoes would help my memory."

"My shout," Lara's hand shot up before any of us could comment. "My way of thanking you all for how welcoming you've been."

"I'll help you carry the food," Jon followed Lara to the van with a picture of hotdogs, curly potatoes, chips, and burgers.

"How long have they been a couple?" I asked, watching their interaction at the food van. I often missed social cues, weirdly, as my journalistic investigative skills were above average.

Seamus shrugged, "I don't think it's anything formal; they just hang out together on weekends."

Lara and Jon returned, arms full of dagwood dogs and twisty potatoes. "Here we are, a feast for us all, or just a snack if you're name's Seamus," Lara quipped. We ate our calorie laden snacks in silence, as we wandered passed the stalls filled with second hand goods, toys, books, videos, puzzles, and home-made goods.

Just as Jon started on his potato on a stick, his mobile rang. "The joys of being one of only two policemen permanently based here," he said as he held the phone up to his ear. "I'll be right there." An ear-splitting bell tone sounded ominously, followed by an equally high-pitched siren.

"A fire in Wynyard Street, that's all the details I have. Fire brigade and ambulance are on their way," Jon tucked his mobile into the pocket of his jacket. "Lara, are you okay to make your own way home?"

"We can give her a lift," Seamus offered before Lara spoke. Jon waved his thanks as he sprinted back to the car park.

"Do we need to tell the others here, about the fire?" Lara asked, "And thanks Seamus, I'd love a lift home."

Seamus looked around the showground. "I don't think we tell anyone. We don't know the details yet; it would only cause anxiety." My stomach didn't need any help, the anxiety causing knots as I thought about the shops I owned in Wynyard Street. Inherited from my parents; I regularly visited the greengrocers, the seamstress, the convenience store, the laundrette and the woodwork store. All were rented, the managers didn't need me, but they appreciated my continued interest. I'd still not forgiven myself for nearly letting a big city conglomerate tear down the businesses and erect a hotel and shopping complex on the site. "I think we should check it out, just to make sure the fire is nowhere near the shops." I was grateful for my friend's mind reading ability.

"Do you mind if I tag along?" Lara asked.

"Not at all, jump in." Seamus unlocked his ute. "We can drop you off later, after dinner at the café." He added hopefully. Lara climbed into the back seat of the twin cab. I took the front passenger seat.

Seamus followed a few other cars whose occupants chose the same time to leave the charity event. "It looks like the event was well attended. I love how our community supports each other." Lara commented. "I'm getting used to seeing fairies and elves wandering around, and the other unusual things that occur from time to time."

Before I could reply that I agreed with her sentiments, we arrived outside the row of shops, or where the row of shops should have been.

My heart sunk to the bottom of my feet, at least that's how it felt. "Oh, my goodness, please tell me it's worse than it looks, and that no one is hurt." My hands shook, as I climbed out of the ute, once Seamus parked it out of the way of the emergency services.

Seamus came around to my side of the truck and placed a steadying hand on my arm. "We'll deal with it together, and I'm sure everyone's okay. It's Sunday afternoon, so only the convenience store would be open." In front of us, five shops should've been standing, welcoming customers, each one painted in a different pastel shade. Instead, charred shells of what used to be, confronted me. Bile rose in my throat.

Lara placed her hand on my other arm. "It mightn't be as bad as it looks," she said reassuringly. I doubted it, but I appreciated the senti-ment.

"Should I ring the tenants?" I wondered aloud. Tear flowed freely down my cheeks. I tasted the salty water as I remembered painting the external weatherboard walls with my father. Now, only charred, burnt wooden frames remained. I doubted anything could be done to save the building.

Jon walked over to where we stood. "This is Stan," he introduced the tall stocky fireman beside him. I wiped the backs of my hands across my cheeks, to get rid of the tears, and did my best to smile at Stan. "He was here a few minutes after the fire started, which burnt hot and quickly. There was nothing his brigade could do to save the building." Jon looked stricken, he may be new to our town, but he cared, which made him a good policeman in my opinion.

Stan cleared his throat. "Jon tells me you own the buildings. You need to know this was deliberate. The fire burnt so ferociously, I expect to find accelerant, like petrol, used to start and spread the fire. All the shops burnt simultaneously. It didn't start in one and spread to the oth-ers. There's nothing left inside the structure to be salvaged. What re-mains will have to be removed, for safety. I'm sorry to have to tell you this." He looked as uncomfortable as Jon at delivering the devastating news.

The acrid smell of burning, wet embers, and fire debris made it difficult to speak without gagging. I steeled my body, demanding it keep the dagwood dog and potato inside my stomach. I could fall apart later, at home. Now I had to be Beth, my parents' advocate, and mayor. "Thank you both, for getting here so quickly and putting out the fire. Let me know what I need to do, who I need to contact. Do I inform the tenants now, or is that something you need to do Jon?" I was aware that both Seamus and Lara stood beside me, ready to support me if I needed it. I'd thank them later. If I turned to either of them now, I'd likely fall apart.

Jon handed me his notebook. "Can you write down the names of your tenants, and if you know their addresses or mobile details off hand, that will come in handy."

I wrote the tenants names down, and their addresses, because somehow that information sat in the recesses of my mind. I grabbed my mobile out of my bag and noted down the mobile numbers I had. "As far as I know, those details should be correct. None of them would have done this though, they don't benefit in any way from losing their businesses." My words caught in my throat as I pictured my parents' friends, now without a source of income. *Later Beth, stay strong.* "According to certain people on council, I'm the one who'd benefit from this, but I didn't start the fire." I steadied my voice and clenched my fists as my anger bubbled just below the surface. "Will you text me when you've spoken to them, I'd like to check in and see how they're doing."

"I can do that. I might need to speak to you again, will you be at home?" Jon asked, looking uncomfortable having to ask me the question.

"Better check Evie's first mate," Seamus piped up. "I'm not saying that I'm hungry, but it's a good place to debrief."

Jon wiped his forehead, smearing a line of black over his fair skin. He turned to Lara. "I'll try to get to the café, if I miss you, I'll catch up with you during the week. This wasn't how I'd planned our day to end. I'd better get going," he added as Stan tapped him on the shoulder.

I watched as the fireman handed Jon something in a bag, wishing I could hear their conversation. Slowly, I became aware of a hand on each of my arms. I reached around covering my friends' hands with my own. "Thank you both for being here," I whispered. I let Seamus and Lara guide me back to the ute, only dragging my eyes off the carnage as we slowly drove away.

Chapter Four

"News travels fast," I commented as we arrived at the café. I'd received several messages on my mobile phone, asking if I was okay, and for details of what had happened in Wynyard Street. Before I could respond to anyone, Evie crossed the floor and embraced me.

I fought the tears threatening to break through my determination. I blinked away the droplets of water that formed in the corners of my eyes. "Whatever you want tonight, is on the house," Evie said as she let me go.

"I appreciate that, but it's not necessary," I responded, touched by her kindness.

"What I think Beth means is, she's had a hard time, as mayor, with people accusing her of taking bribes, acting fraudulently. I don't think she wants anyone to be able to say she burnt down the shops to get more freebies, " Seamus explained, speaking exactly the words on my mind.

Evie squared her shoulders, making her look taller. With her gorgeous purple hair, she didn't exactly project fear into anyone's hearts. "If anyone says that, send them to me. The fairies can be fierce when protecting innocents," she fiercely huffed, before breaking into a smile. "I do understand Beth, anything I can do, just ask. Find a table and I'll come and take your order. Because you're my friend, and I care about you."

A few people I recognised from the community event were seated, munching their way through an assortment of burgers, fries and other café food. Only a few empty tables remained. Lara chose one nearest the kitchen doors. We knew from experience it provided the space to talk freely, with only serving staff able to hear our conversations as they passed by with plates of food. I'd grown to love the sixties ambience of *Evie's Café,* with its colourful checkered tiled floors, red and white fabric on pine tables, chairs and booths, the long bench and high stools for people to use free Wi-Fi, the juke box that played a wide selection of music, and the kids' corner where children could sit and eat independently, while their parents enjoyed a little piece and quiet.

Evie's offered a large range of food, assisted by her parents and some fairies. Seamus knew the menu off by heart. "Let's have chicken wraps, with salad, and chips, and mochas, and a jug of ginger beer," he suggested.

"You not feeling well?" I managed to croak out, "Salad?"

"I thought you'd appreciate that," he grinned. "Means there'll be dessert afterwards." Seamus's loved of food generally was well known throughout Spirit Town.

My mobile beeped, signalling another message. "Do you mind if I check my messages?" I asked.

"Not at all," Lara responded, briefly laying her hand on mine. "I'd be an absolute mess if something happened to my shop. You're holding it together so well."

"Looks can be deceiving," Seamus quipped. I smiled, grateful for his attempt at brevity. I pretended to swipe him with my free hand.

Tears filled my eyes again as I read a message from Jan, who used to own the greengrocer. *I'm with the others, we're all okay. Can we catch up tomorrow morning 9am, my house? Sending love.* I didn't have my work diary with me, but I'd juggle meetings, to make time to see my tenants, and I didn't care what the others on council thought of that. I texted back that 9am was perfect.

Lexi, my assistant at the *Spirit Town Independent*, who'd stepped into my shoes as I took on a term as mayor had tried to call. I read her text. *Oh my gosh, are you okay? Have you got time for a catch up early tomorrow?* I responded, suggested 7am, to which she replied with a thumb's up emoji, followed by a heart and then *if you need anything at all, please let me know.*

I'd been friends with Izzie, who worked at the local radio station, since school. We both moved to the city for university, returning to Spirit Town within a couple of years of each other. *5am coffee your place. Already spoken to Jon. Need anything before then, let me know.* Her hours at the radio meant our coffee catch ups were always early. Early mornings didn't worry me, I love the peace and quiet of the early morning, as the sun began to rise above the horizon.

The other two messages were from Jamie and Greg, both on council with Seamus and I, expressing concern at the news of the fire and offering to change meeting times tomorrow if I needed. Almost as if they were together when they sent their messages. I shook off the feeling of paranoia. I trusted each of the other five council members, to a degree. They'd been cleared of wrongdoing when I discovered Max, our ex-mayor, committed fraud. I responded to both men that I'd be in the office from 10am, so if they could adjust the meetings accordingly, I'd appreciate it.

"I'm tempted to pop my mobile on silent, I won't though, in case Jon or Stan need to talk." I popped my mobile on the table, managing a smile at Seamus and Lara.

"Smart Beth," Seamus commented. "Seriously though, is there anything I should know, in regards to council I mean." When no one else nominated for mayor and I stepped up into the position, Seamus nominated as a member of council, mainly to support me.

"I'm meeting Jan and the others for a cuppa at her house at 9am. Jamie and Greg will push back any meetings until 10am. I'll pop in and see Lexi around 7am, and Izzie will call in at five, on her way to work," I summarised, fidgeting in my chair. I wanted to be doing something, to solve the problem. My common sense told me Jon and Stan were doing what they could, and my only option was to wait.

"Both Lara and I are used to your crazy early morning meetings," Seamus commented. "I know you want to make it right, and that patience is tricky. All you can do is let Jon and Stan do what they need to."

I sensed there he wanted to say more, but Evie arrived at the table with a tray laden with plates of food. "Here you go, I'll bring out the drinks in a second." She lowered her voice and whispered, "Mum overheard a conversation, a customer saw someone near the shops, just before the fire started. She told me as soon as she could, but the customer vanished. I've asked the fairies to keep an eye out for, and to listen for, anything suspicious. I'll keep you updated."

"Thanks Evie. I'd love to say hi to your Mum, if she has a chance. I know she's busy in the kitchen." I resisted the urge to stare at the other patrons to try to work out who could be behind the disaster.

"Is Spirit Town always this full of mysteries?" Lara asked as we picked up our wraps.

I wasn't hungry, I knew I had to eat, still I put my wrap back on its plate. "I've only been back a short time, I would say no, but I suspect Seamus has a different view."

Seamus eyed the food on my plate. "You have to eat something Beth, and this is better than the chocolate and coffee I know will be waiting for you at home." He pretended to frown. "Our little town always has something interesting going on, because we have so many residents with extraordinary abilities. It does appear that in the last year there's been a more sinister element to the events. Totally not related to either of you arriving in town," he added hastily.

"Max engineered a lot of that drama, to line his own pockets, working with the *Castle Home* corporation to build that monstrosity here. It might have brought tourists to our town, but they'd have stayed in that horrible complex, gambling, drinking and buying from their inhouse boutique shops." Lara shuddered at the memory of what our old mayor attempted. He'd paid some teens to cause problems. Luckily, with Jon, the four of us managed to solve that mystery and stop the hotel complex from being built.

True to her word, Evie delivered our hot and cold drinks to the table, apologising for the delay. The three of us ate in silence. I managed to eat most of my wrap. The food settled in my stomach, loosening some of the knots that'd settled there. I wasn't a fan of most takeaways, but Evie's food tasted delicious, and didn't upset my stomach, no matter how many knots it tied itself in.

"It's not a coincidence that this is the third time those shops in Wynyard Street have been targeted." Seamus commented between chips. "First, we had Max and *Castle Home* trying to develop the site, then that Dean Collier and his company – albeit trying to set you up as the person to gain from the development. Does anyone remember the name of Dean's company?"

I sipped my hot drink, letting the bittersweet flavour burst on my taste buds. Evie's mocha reached that perfect balance, every single time. "He's part of a coven. I don't remember the company name." I placed my mug onto the table. "Are you thinking Dean could have set the fire?" It was a definite possibility.

Chapter Five

"I'm sure Jon and Stan will have some leads to follow. They're both good at their job and used to the nuances of Spirit Town." Lara spoke quietly.

As I opened my mouth to speak, a shortish man dressed in green trousers and a jacket, making him look a little like an elf or a leprechaun, approached our table. "You finally did it, didn't you, Ms Mayor," he spat out the words, hand on his hips, leaning towards me.

Seamus jumped out of his seat. "Leave it out Ralph," he said.

The shorter man stared Seamus down. "You're joking! You still have a *thing* for her? After all this time," The angry man said incredulously. "It's not good enough. She gets rid of Max, steps into his job and carries on behaving in the same way. Owns the newspaper, so no independent reporting there."

I clenched my fists under the table, concentrating on keeping my body still. I wanted to jump up and yell at the man. I felt Lara grab my hand under the table. Seamus kept eye contact with the man. "Ralph, I hear you, it's been a bit of a rollercoaster around here lately, but one thing I can assure you is a truth without a doubt. Beth is trustworthy, beyond reproach. She returned to keep her parents' legacy safe. The police will get to the bottom of who set the fire, and why."

I could see Ralph wasn't convinced. After giving Lara's hand a squeeze, I held both my hands out, palms facing up. "Seamus is right, but you have no reason to trust me yet. I will get to the bottom of it, I promise you, even if it means stepping down as mayor." I held his gaze.

Ralph lowered his eyes after a few seconds. "That's a little drastic," he muttered.

"How about a town meeting, so everyone can voice their concerns?" I suggested.

"So long as you don't organise it yourself. Please don't take offense, Madam Mayor, Seamus, but could one of the other councillors coordinate it?" Our interrupter had the good grace to blush at his own words.

Lara faced Ralph, her cheeks also flushed, "Are you saying you don't have faith in Beth or Seamus? Because they are gifted, or is it that they're friends, or maybe because they stepped up to serve our community when others didn't? How do we know you didn't start the fire, to cause trouble?" My heart filled with gratitude for my friend. Lara was quiet, but fiercely loyal.

"Sorry miss, when you put it that way." Ralph looked around a little flustered. Lara moved along on the booth seat and motioned for him to sit down. "I'm one of the men in the men's shed. We lost all our latest creations in that fire. I'm lucky, I have another income source, but for some of the guys, selling their products gave them much needed money. I guess it was being upset that made me speak out of turn." Lara touched his hand, nodding her understanding.

Seamus sat back in his seat next to me. I squeezed his hand under the table. "We're all upset by the fire. We all get emotional. Rather than blaming people, let's wait and see what the authorities find. I've only been back a short while, but I know our community is good at rallying together."

"The saddlery is doing well, and so is the fishing tackle shop. I can donate some funds for the men's shed to buy more wood. If the men are willing to recreate what was lost, I'm happy to sell the products in both shops." Seamus held Ralph's gaze. "You know my dad. Didn't he help with the shed where you store your tools and stuff? If he wasn't travelling, he'd be here pledging his support as well."

As Beth, I wanted to offer assistance, but as mayor I needed to be careful to be seen to be above reproach. "Let's still have that town meeting. Get everyone together and just have a chat. As mayor I've been meaning to host a meeting. We'd tentatively set one for the end of the week. Why don't we ask Lexi to place an article in Tuesday's paper, asking for agenda items?" I was just throwing out ideas, hoping to inspire Ralph's trust. I'd have to run it by the rest of the council at tomorrow's meeting. "If you're willing to give Seamus your contact details, he can coordinate with you."

Ralph nodded, his face returning to normal colour as his anger disappeared. "I apologise again for my outburst. I respected your parents work in this town, yours too Seamus. I'll be in contact after I talk to the guys." He half bowed, tipping an imaginary cap, as he left the table.

I poured three glasses of ginger beer into the tall glasses on the tray next to the jug. "Thanks, both of you, for having my back. I'm just glad Ralph isn't a member of our gifted community, or there'd likely have been an explosion. I could feel his anger when he first confronted us."

"He's an earth elemental, I think." Seamus said. I shot him a puzzled look. I'd heard of those who practiced elemental magic, but I'd not met one in Spirit Town. "I can't remember the name of the city he came from. He arrived years ago, with his wife and sister, I think. They live at the caravan park."

"I read up on magic, years ago, when I first left town. Earth elementals are generally calm, and good with their hands, is that right?" I asked.

"That's part of it," Seamus agreed.

Lara stacked our empty plates and mugs. "There's so much to learn about magic," she whispered, "How do you remember it all? I've met so many customers with some kind of ability, and they don't always know a lot about what they can do. I'd like to be able to help them more."

I found a pen in my pocket, with my phone. I looked up a number and scribbled it on a corner of a paper serviette. "Here's Agnes's mobile number. Have a chat to her. As the convenor of the magic community council, if she doesn't know the answer, she'll know who does."

Lara tucked the number in the pocket of her red woollen dress. "Thanks. I've been meaning to ask Agnes when she's visited the shop, but we end up talking about plants, herbs and lotions and I forget. You've both known her a long time, haven't you?"

"She used to teach us English, in high school. She was intimidating back then, Beth was terrified of her when she first returned to town and had to talk to her as part of the gifted community." Seamus teased.

"I remember," Lara grinned. "Then she gifted you your adorable little kitten," Lara was allergic to most cats, but for some reason Spark's fur didn't cause her to break out in hives.

The doorbell jingled, as Jon walked towards their table. Seamus slid out of his seat, presumably to order more food. "Agnes and I have become friends, though I'd never have thought it possible. It's mutual respect I guess you'd call it." I admitted. Not for one minute would I have believed that Mrs Moggle would have anything but distain for me, her pupil who ran away from her own magic.

Jon slid into the seat vacated by Ralph. His face was drawn, and pale. "You look exhausted," Lara said her voice full of concern.

"It's been a bigger afternoon than I'd planned, that's for sure," he wiped his forehead with the back of his hand.

Seamus returned to his seat. "I've ordered you a coffee, chicken wrap, chips," he told Jon, "and another round of ginger beer and mini mud cakes all round."

Chapter Six

"Thanks mate," Jon said, staring into space for a second, before bringing his focus back to the table. "Stan's report confirms the fire was deliberate. There's evidence petrol was used as an accelerant. One of the eyewitnesses mentioned a man who looked like Max Graham."

"Our old mayor can't be responsible. He made sure he bullied innocent teens into doing his dirty work for him, he'd never get his hands dirty. Plus, he's sitting in gaol somewhere, nowhere near all the money he amassed from his under the table deals." My anger flared at the way Max used a group of our local teens to set fires, destroy the park, and sprawl graffiti around the town. All so he could benefit from a new hotel complex. The teens were scared, because like me as a teen, they didn't know how to control their magic power.

Wiggling my fingers and toes to release the pent-up anger before sparks literally let loose in the café, I stopped speaking as Evie returned with another tray laden with goodies. Behind her, three fairies dressed in gorgeous purple jumpsuits waved little wands that sprinkled tiny stars around her. Children and adults both stared, fascinated at the sight. I sipped my fresh glass of ginger beer, marvelling at how Evie's food and drink never upset my stomach, or caused anyone with any allergies discomfort. Could the fairies in part, help keep people emotions and moods calm? One of the fairies made eye contact with me and smiled.

Before I'd a chance to ask Seamus about that, Jon cleared his throat. "About Max, I had Fred make some calls when we returned to the station. It appears Max served less than two months of a five-year sentence. Some fancy lawyer appealed that he'd made those decisions under duress and that he wasn't to blame. I'm very grateful my bosses decided to have Fred stay on here for a while," he added. Fred, one of the extra resources during the debacle with Max, expressed interest in staying on, if needed.

I took a sharp breath in, slowly releasing it, as all three of my dinner companions eyed me with concern. "Did any of the board members of *Castle Home* end up in goal?" I asked, certain I knew the answer.

Jon shook his head. "No. That company has dissolved, all the hotel complexes built have been rebranded to *Majestic Mirage.* The board members appear to have disappeared, not dead, changed their names and moved onto other projects. I'm sorry Beth. I'm not sure I believe Max is behind this, but just in case I think you need to be careful."

"I'm okay," I told my friends, as all three sets of eyes searched my face for signs of a meltdown. "I know I can be emotional, anxious, but now I'm angry. At Max or whoever started the fire that burnt down the Wynyard Street shops leaving five tenants without a source of income." I sipped my drink, to steady the ideas spinning around in my head. "As Beth the person, and as mayor, there are things I can do and focus on. The community meeting, making sure Ralph and the others find alternative income sources, or new locations for their businesses, and are paid for the loss of their stock. Once I get home, I'll make a list."

"Oh no, not one of your infamous lists!" Seamus mocked, holding his stomach as if I'd delivered a blow. "We all know what that means," he grinned.

I grinned back, "As I was saying," I continued, drawing my body up tall in my seat, "I'll make a list of everything I can do." I turned to Jon, "I know you'll keep me informed, as mayor and as the owner of the properties, and please don't hesitate to tell me if you think it's Max. I won't try and contact him." I stretched my fingers out, letting the seething anger ripple away harmlessly. A fairy hovering near the children's corner nodded in appreciation as the energy evaporated as it encountered a flutter of fairy dust. "For now, let's try these amazing looking mini mud cakes." I chose one of the cakes, with chocolate chips ensconced in rich chocolate icing and took a bite. I tasted a hint of peppermint amid the layers of velvety chocolate. "Delicious."

An elderly lady, with her grey hair piled high on her head in a bun, her glasses perched on her nose, carrying a patchwork library bag entered the café. "Agnes! How lovely to see you," I jumped up and gave my old teacher a quick hug. No longer scared of her, I respected her and considered her a mentor, though that word didn't cover the depth of our connection.

Jon jumped up, offering Agnes a seat. "Jon, thank you, but no, I won't stay long. Lara, Seamus," she nodded at the others. "I'm glad you're here with Beth." She faced me, lowering her voice, "I wanted to offer you my condolences, and a warning. Things are not what they seem. I've had a strange afternoon, visited by a couple of departed friends, one convinced me to consult my cards, which I did. The cards were clear, you must be careful. Hidden forces are at play here." She shook her head a little. "I hate sounding like some two-bit fortune teller, but the cards never lie. I only ever resort to them when needs must. Unfortunately, they didn't tell me exactly who or what you must look out for."

"We've some ideas," Seamus's voice was quiet, a sign that anger simmered below the surface. My friend didn't anger easily, but when he did, I listened, and so should everyone else. "We'll make sure no harm comes to Beth."

"I know that young Seamus," Agnes spoke to him like we were back in high school, but with a level of respect I rarely heard her use with anyone so young. "Jon, you have reinforcements coming." It was a statement, not a question. "Don't discount any clues, especially if they appear unlikely." She reached into her patchwork bag and handed a book to Lara. "I'll call in tomorrow, I've a task and I'd like you to assist me."

Agnes reached back into her bag and pulled out a chain with a small metal key attached. She handed it to me. "This is yours. Beryl gave it to me for safe keeping years ago. The key opens her journal." She stopped speaking, glancing around the café as a cold breeze made the hairs on the back of my neck stand on end. The looks on the others at the table told me they felt the same. I quickly pocketed the chain. Agnes nodded her approval. Speaking in a much louder voice she added, "If the town meeting goes ahead on Friday, the council will attend. We need to show Ralph and the others that they have our support. Thank you for including us." Without waiting for a response, Agnes turned and left the café, her long purple shirt giving the impression she floated out the door.

"Is she always that intense?" Jon asked.

I looked at Seamus, curious as to his take on what just happened. "Something's rattled her, which I didn't think was possible to be honest. The most formidable woman I know." That he didn't add *worse than Beth* told me her words concerned him. He looked at me, adding, "We do need to heed the warning, I'm not saying you need a police escort, but lock your doors, brush up on your protection enchantments, don't walk outside in the dark, or work late alone at the office. Be sensible."

My brain was going to burst if I didn't soon get to make lists of everything that had happened, that I needed to do over the next couple of days. Evie's clock told me it was nearly seven in the evening. I yawned, no wonder I felt tired. "Is the clock on the right time? The last time I checked my watch I swear it said three thirty."

"We were at Wynyard Street for ages, longer than you'd think. We arrived here around five, I remember thinking how busy the café was for that time of day. Then there was Ralph. How did Agnes know about him and the meeting?" Lara's words tumbled out. I reached for her hand.

Jon's mobile buzzed on the table. He peered at the screen. "I'm needed at the station. If there's anything that seems odd, at home, or at work, anything at all, doesn't matter what time, you call me." Jon's hand on my shoulder had a steadying effect. "I'll be in touch tomorrow mid-morning."

"Thanks Jon, if I don't answer, I'll ring you back as soon as I can." I watched as our friend walked towards the door, shoulders tall, on duty, his aura, giving away his weariness. Could he be an empath and not know it? Probably. I'd never asked Jon about his heritage.

"He's from the city originally," Seamus answered my thoughts. "Jon applied for the role here when Detective Murray retired earlier this year. I haven't had a chance to ask him about his family or connection to Spirit Town."

Lara yawned. "Excuse me," she said. "I know you read each other's minds, Seamus more so than you. It's such a weird sensation, I'm sure Agnes knew the question I wanted to ask her, about magic."

"It is weird, and annoying at times," I pretended to frown at my mind reader, "But it's also pretty cool, and living here, you'll get used to it. I'm glad Agnes sees a kindred spirit in you, she's different with you, more comfortable, let's her guard down. I'm babbling," I yawned, covering my mouth with my hand.

Seamus stood. "Time to get you both home."

The three of us caught Evie's eye and waved. As we left the café, three young teens entered, laughing at something one of them said. "Evie works such long hours," Lara commented. "So do her parents, I'm tired now and I'm half their age. I don't know how Bert and Bessie do it, cooking and serving all day."

"It's their passion," Seamus replied. "They don't see it as a job. They live above the café, always have. There's a rooftop garden that I suspect is enchanted and managed for the most part by fairies. All the fresh food is grown and harvested there, all year around."

"How did I not know that? I suspect there is a lot I don't know about Spirit Town and its residents. I don't suppose there's a book I can read?" My comment was serious. I loved to read, and it might be a way of remembering and knowing everything I needed to.

Seamus pressed the button on his key fob, unlocking the doors on his ute. "I've not heard of one but maybe check the library. If we had one, that's where it'd be."

I opened my mouth to answer Seamus, but just at that moment a bright light flashed, right in front of us.

Chapter Seven

Seamus had parked in front of *The Magic Shop,* finding an empty spot there when we'd headed to the café. Less cars remained on the main street now, most people would've gone home to prepare for the week ahead. I blinked rapidly, trying to clear the residue spots of light in my line of sight.

Lara pointed to the walkway beside the shop. "Did anyone else see movement there?"

"All I can see are darn spots in front of my eyes," Seamus muttered. A second smaller flash lit up the interior of the shop. I closed my eyes quickly and opened them again. More spots of light.

"Should we investigate?" I asked the occupants of the ute, doubting that any of us felt like leaving the relative safety of the vehicle.

"Normally I'd say yes, but let's leave it to the experts." Seamus grumbled, "I still can't see enough to drive."

Lara's fingers flew over the keypad on her mobile. "For some reason I can see fine. I sent a message to Jon, asking him to meet us here."

I tried to remember what I knew about the owners of the shop in front of us. "Does anyone know if the owners are likely to be at work this late?"

"There's a back room, where people meet, for seances and tarot readings. I thought it was a tongue in cheek thing, all smoke and mirrors, and not real magic. The owners are new, only arrived here after our last festival." Lara offered. "At least that's what I've been able to glean from customers."

Seamus moved in his seat, so he faced Lara in the back. "I've not been able to find any information about them," he admitted. "There's even debate about the names of the owners. I've met them, once. Magda and Marcia, but then I hear them referred to as Sable and Serene. I swear it's the same two women, but with different names."

"How odd. It sounds like smoke and mirrors, as you said Lara, they don't want us to know who they are or what they're doing." The light spots blocking my vision were beginning to fade, leaving behind a headache. "I can't see any movement, inside or outside now."

"Me either, oh look, here's Jon now." The familiar police sedan pulled up beside Seamus's door.

"Is everything okay?" he asked as the three of us tentatively exited the ute.

"I'm not sure," Seamus replied. "We hopped in the ute to head home, and a bright light flashed inside the shop." He pointed to the store window where a small light illuminated magic kits, a top hat, a white rabbit and a magician's wands. Kids toys, or so I thought. "There was a second flash, and Lara thought she saw something move in the walkway to the side, but there's been nothing for a few minutes now."

The hairs on the back of my neck hackled, as we stood looking at the shop façade. "Do you want us to stay, and help you check it out?" I asked not feeling as brave as my words but hating the thought of leaving Jon alone.

"Fred's meeting me here in a few minutes, but thanks for asking. I don't suppose any of you have contact details for the shop owners?" he asked, taking out his notebook hopefully.

I shook my head, "No, we were just talking about that. Apart from the fact they've only been here a couple of months, none of us know any details." I covered my mouth as another yawn escaped.

Seamus tapped the door of the ute. "If you're sure you're okay, I'm dropping these lovely ladies home, it's been a long day and I'm sure we all have an early start, though not as early as Beth's."

"I might be worn, but I'm stronger than I look," Jon managed a grin. "Also, I'm trained for this sort of stuff."

"I know you'll keep us informed, let's book in a tentative catch up tomorrow lunchtime." Seamus shrugged at the look I gave him. "I'm not hungry now, just thinking ahead, planning, like you do. We gotta eat and stay caffeinated." Laughing, we said our goodnights to Jon, and hopped back into Seamus's ute.

Lara lived in Little Street, a couple of blocks from Tumble Street, the main street in Spirit Town. "Your little cottage suits you perfectly," I said as we pulled up in front of a white picket fence, behind which stood a white panelled cottage with two windows and a wooden front door facing the street.

"Thank you," Lara smiled. "I was fortunate that it was a package deal with the business. If it wasn't so late, I'd invite you in."

"Next time," I agreed. "We don't always have to meet at mine."

"I know, goodnight. I'll see you tomorrow." Lara hopped out, Seamus waited until she'd unlocked her door, turned on the lights and shut the front door before driving away.

We drove the rest of the way in silence. "Do you want me to stay tonight - in Grandma's room?" he asked as we pulled into my driveway.

A large part of my brain, or maybe my heart, wanted to scream *YES*. Instead, I found myself responding with, "I'll be fine, by myself, I have Spark, and Buddy," I added.

Seamus raised his eyebrows. "What use is the orphan sheep who lives in your backyard and saves you from having to mow going to be if there's an intruder or malevolent magic?"

"Not much," I admitted, "but Spark is my familiar, Agnes gave him to me, he protects me, and he'd alert me to any danger."

"And lick the bad guy to bits with his tiny sandpaper tongue?" Seamus sounded doubtful. He sighed. "I know better than to try to argue with you about who's most stubborn in this friendship. If you promise to ring me if you hear so much as a leaf fall off a tree, or a mouse scurry on the floorboards on the verandah," Seamus spoke firmly, though I heard the concern in his voice.

I leaned over and hugged my oldest, bestest friend. "Thank you, for being here for me, for being awesome. I promise I'll ring if there's anything." I hopped out of the ute, before I changed my mind and invited Seamus inside. I knew he watched me as I unlocked the door and turned on the hall light. I locked the door behind me. He'd wait until I'd time to check all the rooms for any hidden intruders, and only after he saw the light in the kitchen on, where he knew I'd be boiling the kettle and sitting writing my lists would he drive away.

I sent a quick text, after assessing the house was free of danger, telling him it was all clear and he could head home. So close sending an alternate text, inviting him in, I dropped my phone next to my laptop and picked up my familiar, who'd greeted me at the door and followed me from room to room. "Hey little guy, did you miss me? I sure missed you. What a day. You must be starving." I kissed his forehead and returned him to the floor. I dropped a handful of dried cat food into his bowl, adding water to his water bowl. I poured hot water into my mug of coffee, added some cold milk, and sat at the kitchen table.

Only last week, I'd rearranged the old dining room to accommodate an office space for me. It seemed such a long time ago. I considered moving into the office to make my lists, but I'd an early start in the morning and it'd be easier if everything I needed was in one place. "It's horrible Spark," I told my kitten as he walked around my ankles. "Someone burnt the Wynyard Street shops to the ground." I lifted him to my lap, my eyes brimmed with tears as I spoke aloud in the silence. "After all Mum and Dad did for the community. Whether it's Max, or Dean or someone else, I'll find out and they'll pay for it." Spark patted my cheek with his paw, reminding me to calm down, lest sparks literally escaped and flew around the space. "More importantly," I added, "We need to make sure Jan, Brett, Tanya, and the others have a way to make an income." My kitten wrapped himself into a ball on my lap as I jotted down some notes. I transferred my to-do-list onto my laptop.

Chapter Eight

I must've nodded off at the dining room table. A little sandpaper tongue licking my cheek woke me. I woke to my kitten licking my cheek. "Hi little fella," I lifted him onto my lap. I wiggled my laptop mouse; its digital clock informed me the new day had begun. "Just after midnight," I groaned aloud, as I kicked off my shoes, slipping on my fluffy slippers I'd left on the floor earlier in the day. It felt like a lifetime ago. I plodded my way to my room, changing out of my clothes and into a pair of pink flannel pyjamas. I yawned as I surveyed my room. I wasn't sure what I hoped to find.

Spark nudged my pile of clothes. "I'll pick them up in the morning," I told him. He persisted. I bent and picked up the clothes. As I folded my jeans I felt a lump in the pocket. "The key!" I exclaimed, "I forgot all about this," I held the key on its chain out for my familiar to sniff it. "Do you know where Grandma hid her journal?" I asked him hopefully. "Maybe I could tune in to her in my dreams," I ran to the kitchen, checking the back door lock, before turning off the light. After checking the front door, I hopped into bed, pulled up my covers, and turned off my bedside light.

My grandma, and my parents, had visited me during my dreams before, passing on messages, and words of encouragement. Totally random, it wasn't like I'd tried to channel them, or to connect directly them. My bond with Grandma had always been strong. My early years were spent following her around, hanging on to her every word. When she died, I spent the rest of my childhood missing her. Until Seamus told me, I'd no idea she'd wanted to teach me the old ways, that my parents had forbade her. With Grandma I learnt about plants, and crystals, reading, and fairytales. I watched her cook, though I didn't inherit any of her skill in that area.

Since returning home, it took me ages to get the nerve to enter my parents' and grandma's room. I'd only braved it recently, with Seamus's help. I didn't remember seeing a journal, but I wasn't looking for it. "It'll be quicker if I contact her and she tells me where it is," I murmured to Spark, as he curled up on my blanket.

I tossed, moving my blankets, squeezing my eyes shut, asking sleep to come take me to Grandma. I opened my eyes a tiny bit, closing them quickly, as my bedside clock advised me I'd been in bed less than half an hour. It was going to be a long night. "Is there a spell or a chant I can say, to call Grandma?" I didn't expect Spark to answer. I wriggled over until I could reach the key I'd placed on my bedside. I wiggled some more, until I sat against my pillows. "Grandma, Agnes gave me the key for your journal. I don't want to pry, but there may be something in it that will help. While I'm talking, Mum, Dad, I'm sorry, but the shops in Wynyard Street burnt down. You probably know that already."

Talking to ghosts! What next? Reading tarot cards. I laughed at my thoughts. *You're tired Beth, get some sleep.* I yawned and snuggled back under the blankets. Izzie would be knocking on my door for a cuppa, in less than four hours.

The familiar sensation, of sitting with my parents and my grandma, made me open my eyes. This wasn't a dream. We were sitting at the table on the verandah in the moonlight. I knew they were ghosts; the fuzzy outline of their bodies gave it away. "I'm so sorry about the shops," my voice caught in my throat. I wanted to embrace them, to hug them and never let go, but I wasn't sure of the protocol with spirits.

A feeling of warmth spread through my body. I saw that fuzzy light that outlined my spirit family spread around me, like an otherworldly hug. A gentle beeping woke me up. I didn't remember setting my alarm for 4:30am. I lay still for a few moments, savouring the warmth surrounding me. I closed my eyes, trying for a final glimpse of my family. The beeping continued. I angled myself up onto my elbow, to reach the button to switch off the alarm. Spark jumped off the bed, looking behind at me to make sure I followed him.

"Okay, okay, I'm coming," I swung my legs out of bed and joined Spark in the kitchen. I scooped some food into his bowl, filled the kettled and headed for the shower.

Less than five minutes later I'd dressed in black pants, a red shirt, and black shoes. My jacket hung over the kitchen chair that held my laptop bag. "It's easier to get organised for work, now that you can stay here during the day." I considered my words. If there was danger, as Jon implied, Spark should spend the day with Lexi. When I became mayor, he'd been too little to leave at home, and Lexi offered to mind him, at the newspaper office. Their strong bond didn't affect Lexi's work. "Luckily, we left pretty much everything you need at the office. You'll have such fun with Lexi today," I crooned, my decision made.

I pulled out two mugs, one with cats, the other with horses. Izzie and I purchased them together at a school fete a long time ago. She kept the bird and dog mugs. Mum and Dad kept the mugs, along with the colourful mugs Seamus and I always used. A large spoonful of coffee in each mug, I turned the kettle on to boil again, as Izzie banged on the door.

"Check before you open the door!" Izzie admonished me at the same time as she enveloped me in a hug. A little taller than me, her long dark curly hair hung loose, tickling my nose.

"Hi Izzie! Great to see you too!" I grinned, as Spark jumped up on his hind legs to say hi to our friend.

"What's going on girlfriend?" she asked as we headed to the kitchen, arm in arm.

I poured some hot water in the mugs, adding a splash of milk in both. "Someone burnt down the shops in Wynyard Street." I heard my voice waver. "A witness named Max Graham, which apparently is possible, because a fancy pants lawyer successfully argued for his release from prison." I plonked myself at the table, Izzie did the same. "Dean Collier, or some other person who doesn't like me as mayor, is probably involved, so it's likely I'll be accused of setting the fire myself." I sipped the soothing black liquid. "How about you?"

"My life is boring, compared to you, just the way I like it," she said. "I'd rather live vicariously through you. The only gift my parents gifted me with, is the gift of the gab."

"Oh Izzie, I love you!" I smiled properly for the first time since the fire. "You know your radio station is such a great way to keep the residents informed and up to date. It's such a great service. You help Lexi and I all the time, and others as well."

Izzie watched me over the rim of her mug, smiling as she ran her finger along the horses on her mug. "I like helping people. I love that my talking shines a light on issues. How can I help you? Do you want to speak on the radio, defend yourself? We both know if it's Max or Dean behind this, they'll be spreading lies."

"Thanks. I appreciate it. I don't want to make it about me, as the owner of the shops. I'd like to approach it a little differently and host that community meeting I spoke about last week. Would you be willing to promote the town meeting on the radio? Ask residents who have questions for me as mayor to send their questions into the council email address. I want to make it clear that while I'm willing to answer everyone's questions, the focus of the meeting will be finding new ways for the tenants to make a living, making sure they aren't out of pocket, which I'm hoping insurance will cover but you know what I mean." My arms ached as I held my mug to my lips. Was I coming down with a cold? I couldn't afford to be sick.

Chapter Nine

As she put her mug down, Izzie considered my comments. She had a way of frowning, as she thought through what she'd been told and how she'd respond. It made her a brilliant reporter. Her behaviour unsettled quite a few guests to her radio show. I'd been sitting in the waiting room, watching through the glass as her interviewee sat trembling, waiting to see what next question would be thrown at them. "You only hear the people who are out to tarnish your name. There are many people who support you as mayor, and as you, Beth Harriott. I respect that you want to keep yourself out of the spotlight, that it's about the tenants. There'll be questions, people are curious. If you ask for questions from the community, I'm assuming you'll have responses ready for whatever queries come up."

"Yes, I'd planned for that, during the Dean Collier debacle, I penned draft responses to all the questions I received about my motives, my ethics, why I stepped up as mayor. My answers will be pretty much the same. I'm expecting the questions will be similar, though I'm hoping no one makes it look like I had anything to do with happened to the Wynyard Street shops..." My voice cracked. I swallowed hard, as my throat burned. "Sore throat, I think I'm coming down with something."

With her fingers out in front in the shape of a cross Izzie yelped, "Stay away from me, I can't afford to get sick."

"Me either," I responded, as I grabbed supplements from the medicine shelf in the pantry. I popped some echinacea, vitamin C and turmeric into my mouth, swallowing the concoction with a drink of water. "It's normally my stomach or migraine that tell me I'm stressed, or anxious." Maybe I'm run down from all the recent events. "So yes, I've answers for all the likely questions, and I'll stand by my last resort, that I'll step down if people consider me corrupt. I only stepped up because no one else would. I'd happily go back to work with Lexi at the paper."

Izzie looked at her watch. "More people support you than you realise. Thanks for the cuppa, I've got to head in for a production meeting. Is it public knowledge, about Max? Can I say he's no longer in gaol?"

"I guess so, and that he's been seen in Spirit Town. Heck, I don't even care if you want to mention Dean Collier." I walked Izzie to the door, Spark in her arms where he'd plonked himself as soon as she'd sat down. "Do you know any details about *The Magic Shop?* Who owns it? There is something odd about it."

Izzie turned around, "Oh, what have you heard?"

"Nothing, I'm just curious, I haven't met them." I shooed her out the door as I realised I'd piqued her interest. Izzie opened her mouth, ready to ask me more questions. "Don't be late to your meeting on my account. I appreciate your support with this. If I learn anything interesting about the shop, not just my spider senses, I'll let you know."

"Good. You know I can't resist a good mystery. Who'd have thought that a lot of the mystery going on in town would involve you though? I mean what's with that? Your parents and gran didn't have this sort of thing going on, did they?" Izzie responded. I knew that look, she would remember this conversation and bring it up another day. I bit my tongue, wanting to tell her, but knowing she'd stay, ask questions, and be super late for work.

I waved as Izzie hopped in her black jeep, its cloth roof was rarely closed, except for early morning drives to work. "That's a story for another day. I'm discovering that life here isn't as uncomplicated as it seemed, growing up." I grinned at Izzie's open mouth as she started the vehicle, wishing we'd longer to chat. Both committed to our careers, our work ethic remained a common bond, since working together on a science project in junior high school. Finding a love of animals and of sharing information, in print and the spoken word, meant we'd remained friends through adult life.

My familiar tugged at my trouser leg. I noticed a piece of paper stuck under the coarse haired welcome mat. "How did that get there?" I asked Spark, as I bent to pick up what I imagined to be a piece of my notepad. I dropped it as quickly as I picked it up, scooping my hand down to catch it before it slipped down the steps. The words *YOU WERE WARNED* screamed at me in old newspaper print, crudely glued on the page. I pinched the paper between my fingertips as I took it inside to find a plastic bag. Sealing the page in a snap-lock bag I slipped it into my bag, meaning to ask Jon to check it for fingerprints. "When and who Spark? I didn't see the paper there last night, but it was dark. I seem to be collecting a few enemies. I'm glad you'll be with Lexi today. I'd be sad if they burned the house down," my voice caught at the thought of losing all the family history and memories, "but I'd be devastated if I lost you too."

I reached into the crisper and took out a carrot and an apple. Spark skipped behind me as I opened the back door. Buddy, the orphaned lamb, now a sheep greeted me at the bottom of the steps. His brown and white wool a little damp in the morning dew. "Hey Buddy," I held out the carrot, which he took and munched. "I'm sorry, but I can't take you with me today. I'll talk to Seamus about whether you can stay on the farm, just until we get to the bottom of whatever this is. I don't want anything happening to you." Buddy nudged the hand containing the apple. I opened my palm, and he took the piece of fruit. "I don't know how late I'll be tonight," I told him, rubbing the wool on his back. It left my hand a little tacky. "I love you fella." I told him, patting him again, hesitant to leave him alone. *Don't be silly Beth, he'll be fine, remember it's not about you.*

I locked the kitchen door, after washing my sticky hands in the kitchen sink. I wiped the sink out with paper towel and ran the water to wash up the mugs in the sink. After drying my hands for a second time, I rummaged in the fridge for breakfast. "This will have to do," I told Spark as I found the remaining few strawberries and an orange. I managed to eat half the orange, as I sat and scrolled through my emails. I liked to be prepared as best I could for the day ahead. The knots in my stomach returned as I remembered I couldn't simply duck to Wynyard Street to pick up more fruit and veg and a cake for Seamus.

As I closed the lid on the laptop my gaze fell on the pantry cupboard. Dad built it and replaced the old fridge with a new stainless steel one after I left home. The rest of the kitchen was as I remembered it as a child, sitting with Grandma at this table. A country cottage style, at least fifty, probably sixty years old. Grandma built the house, so the story went, and updated it when my mother was pregnant with me. The cupboards were a sturdy wood, painted white. The benchtops made from a dark wood whose name escaped me. The double sink was deeper than most, and white rather than stainless. The kitchen table and chairs were a light pine hue. I walked over to the original pantry. Grandma and I would sit on a stool amongst the bags of flour and sugar, shelves behind us filled with jars and packets of food. She'd read me stories, recipes, fairytales, whatever books were around. In her memory my parents created a little reading room in the small space, adding a brighter light bulb, and a mirror which provided the illusion that the area was bigger. I pulled the string to turn on the light. Where jars and packets of dried food once sat, books now lined those same handmade, rough, splintered wood shelves. Some books were favourites of my parents, I'd added to the collection since arriving home. I ran my hand along the tops of the books. Did I accidentally give away Grandma's journal when I donated a heap of books to the second-hand shop?

Spark tapped my leg, breaking me from my brain whirl. "True, it is more likely to be hidden in Grandma's room. It can stay there for now." I headed back to my bedroom, gently lifting the key and its chain from where I'd been clutching it under my pillow in an effort to find answers. I lifted my pillows, half expecting to find an answer hidden underneath. My heart beat loudly in my chest as an amethyst heart, no bigger than my fingernail lay there, glistening in the sunlight that peeked through my blinds. My hand flew to the dainty gold chain, on which sat a similar sized gold heart. A present from beyond the grave from my grandmother. I carefully unclasped my necklace, added the amethyst heart, and returned the necklace to my neck. *Thank you* I whispered aloud to Grandma, Mum and Dad, certain that one of them, or all, had somehow reached through the veil and placed it there.

Chapter Ten

The clock hadn't struck 7am, yet when I opened the door, I knew Lexi would've been at work for a while. "Beth!" Lexi jumped up from behind her desk and embraced me. Her dark hair tied in two plaits that stuck out either side of her head made her look even younger than her late twenties. Her tartan black and white dress was simple. She held me at arm's length. "Are you okay? Did you get any sleep at all? Oh Spark, hi! Thanks for coming to keep me company today." She scooped up my kitten, snuggling him into the crook of her arm. "You're such a clever kitten, walking into work like a grown up." It'd been easy to train Spark to follow me into work. He was a quick learner.

"Hi Lexi, thanks for meeting me so early, for looking after Spark and for being awesome! I've spoken to Izzie. I don't want this mess to be about me, Beth the person, who lost the shops, or me as mayor. This story must be about Jan and the others who've lost their livelihood. I'm going ahead with the town meeting this Friday, with a focus on helping the tenants each find alternate sources of income. Please ask residents with ideas, or any questions for me as mayor, to send them in to make sure I answer them on the day." I stopped, drawing in a breath and exhaling. I knew she'd make sense of my babble.

Lexi ducked into the little kitchenette and returned with a takeaway cup and a paper bag. "From Evie's," she held the goodies out to me. Most mornings, before I became mayor, Lexi would greet me when I arrived at the paper, with a takeaway cuppa and a paper bag with a raspberry and white chocolate muffin.

"Thank you," I took the goodies from Lexi, and sipped the mocha I loved so much. "I know you're more than capable of running things here single handedly, the best employee ever, but do you want me to look at anything before I head into the office? I've some time to spare, and I'm meeting Jan and the others at nine. Which gives us two hours if you need me."

"The fire will be the lead story. Any ideas you can share on who started it?" She sat back behind her computer, fingers poised at the keyboard.

"Several ideas, no evidence yet but some things you can print. Max Graham is now a free man. Released when a lawyer from the city argued his case. A witness identified Max at the scene of the fire. Dean Collier is another option. *Castle Home* has rebranded to *Majestic Mirage*...On a not necessarily unrelated note, I want to know more about the people who own *The Magic Shop*. There's something a little off about them." I took a breath, and started eating my muffin as Lexi's fingers flew across her keyboard.

"Have Jon, or Stan provided any solid evidence?" She asked over the top of her monitor.

"Stan's report stated that the fire was deliberate, accelerant used in all the shops. I expect to hear from Jon today sometime. I'll provide you an update as soon as I have one. I'll email you and Izzie the details for the town meeting on Friday. Can you give me until lunchtime for that information?"

"Sure," Lexi hopped off her chair and picked up Spark, nuzzling her face in his fur. "I'm going to take some quality time with this little guy, then get the paper ready for the printer. Just keep me updated when you can. Now go, and get done what you have to, we have it all covered here."

I looked around the office. Lexi rarely used my actual office, preferring instead to use the desk at the front counter, so she could more easily interact with clients. She used the conference room if she needed more space. Dad built most of the wooden furniture, when my parents bought the business. With his craftsmanship in each room, it felt like an extension of home. I missed working with Lexi on the paper, but I knew she managed quite well on her own. She'd a real knack for getting people to open up about themselves.

"Being mayor isn't forever," Lexi nudged me. "You'll be back here in no time, I mean, after your term is up. Don't let people like Max or Dean make you step down. So many people are happy with what you are doing as mayor."

I hugged Lexi, nearly squashing Spark, who wriggled in her arms. "Thank you," I whispered. "I'll be in touch, before midday if possible." I left the office, familiar tears welling as the emotions of the last twenty-four hours caught me.

There was time to duck into work, before meeting Jan, or I could grab some food for morning tea. I knew Jan would have baked, but I needed to buy something, for each of my tenants. I drove past the council chambers, heading instead for the supermarket. I parked just across from the two-dollar shop, next to the supermarket. *The Cheap Shop,* as it was named, offered six baskets outside on special for two dollars each. I bought the whole lot, took them to my car, and returned to the super-market.

Paying attention to my intuition I collected a selection of chocolates, biscuits, cheese, grapes and berries, fancy bubbly flavoured water, and other bits and pieces for each tenant. Remembering Buddy, I retraced my steps and grabbed a packet of apples and another of carrots. In the bakery section I collected a couple of cakes and some lamingtons. The hairs on the back of my neck prickled.

I looked around, expecting to see Dean, or Max, but the only customers in view were two mothers with young children pushing trolleys, and an older couple carrying a basket. No one in my sight posed a threat. Intuition told me the unseen threat was dangerous; in a way I'd not yet figured out. Three elves pushing a cart piled high with baked goods distracted me. I admired their bright red pants and orange shirts, with little flowers stitched along the seams. The muffins, cupcakes, and packets of slice lined the cardboard shelves in the shape of a tree.

The clock above the deli advised me I'd thirty minutes to get to Jan's house. With one checkout open, I opted for the self-serve area and swiped my items through the register. Concentrating on the beep of the machine, I jumped as a finger tapped me on the shoulder.

I spun around, expecting to be face to face with Max or Dean. The space was empty. A shiver ran down my spine. I turned back to the machine, ignoring the second tap on my shoulder. *I'm safe, no one can hurt me, I'm safe, I'm powerful just as I am.* Did I remember the chant from sitting on Grandma's knee? Serenity swept over me, enveloping me in a hug, that reminded me of Grandma. Placing my groceries back into the trolley I quickly headed for my car. The car park had filled up in the time I'd been inside. All kinds of cars, trucks, and SUVs lined up in the parking spaces. The noise of the babbling toddlers was somehow reassuring. Mothers admonishing their children made life seem normal, safe, not filled with magic and mystery. I dismissed the taps on my shoulder as a result of lack of sleep.

Chapter Eleven

I walked into a sombre gathering, on Jan's front verandah. Brett, Mike, Jan, Tanya, Mary, and Ralph were seated around two white wrought iron tables. A large blue teapot, with eight matching cups sat on a tray. Shortbread biscuits sat on one plate, melting moments on the other. I added a chocolate mud cake and a packet of lamingtons to the table.

Tears flowed freely down my cheeks as I whispered, "I'm sorry." Jan hugged me first, then Tanya and Mary. Brett and Mark nodded from their seats around the table. "I have something in my car." I inhaled and exhaled a couple of times as I took the now full baskets out of my car, handing one to each of the people around the table. "This is just a little something...there are no words..." I couldn't think of anything to say that would be suitable.

"It wasn't your fault," Jan spoke sternly. "We all agree on that." She stared at each person around the table, each nodded their agreement. "Spending time on what ifs and moaning won't help us. We must work out how we're going to move forward."

The ivy growing around Jan's verandah created a feeling of a secret hide out, like something out of one of the books I read as a teenager. Climbing roses and geraniums in pots added to the ambiance. "Seamus and I have some ideas. We're hoping the community may have some other options. There'll be a town meeting on Friday. The focus will be on finding each of you alternate sources of income, I'll answer any questions that come up about my role as mayor. Can I help with anything right now?"

Ralph shuffled in his chair. "I must apologise for yesterday afternoon. Being upset is no excuse for how I spoke."

"I understand how emotions can make us do and say things we don't mean, please don't worry about that, it's forgotten," I managed a smile as I met his eyes.

Jan held up the teapot. "Do you have time for tea, cake, biscuits, and conversation? I know you are busy Beth, we appreciate you joining us."

Just under an hour later, I pulled up into the closest car spot to the council chambers. I didn't want to be late, knowing they'd already changed the time to suit me. My stomach was so full of morning tea treats, my heart full of emotions, all I wanted to do was sit and organise my emails and my dairy. A tall, broad-shouldered man met me at the door, holding it open for me. "Good morning, Beth."

"Jamie, hello, thank you for getting the door. I hope I'm not late for the meeting." I juggled my laptop and my jacket as I opened the door to the mayors' office.

"We're set up in the conference room, and no, you're not late, five minutes to spare, if you want to make a cuppa." Jamie never smiled, but his voice carried a softer tone than last time we spoke.

"Thanks, I'm fine with water, I'll follow you." I pulled my laptop out of my bag, hung my jacket on the back of my chair and walked behind Jamie the short distance to the larger meeting room. I nodded hello to the councillors seated around the large table, grabbing a water bottle from the fridge in the corner before sitting in one of the vacant chairs. Seamus sat directly opposite me, with Greg and Jamie on one side, Kim and Glen on the other. We were all similar in age, give or take a few years, Seamus and I were the newcomers, the others having served with Max, and all been cleared of any inappropriate behaviour. I wasn't entirely convinced of their innocence, and I knew they trusted me as much as I trusted them. A few months into my new role, and still every meeting felt like an uncomfortable job interview.

I opened my water bottle and drank the cooling liquid as I looked each person in the eye. "Thanks for changing the meeting time, I appreciate it." I started strong, not letting my insecurities get in the way of the job at hand. "I know this meeting is to discuss the developments in the area, specifically the proposed agricultural teaching facility and the new farming techniques, and I'm keen for the updates. Firstly, I want to address the elephant in the room. The fire at the Wynyard Street shops. Deliberately lit according to the fire chief's report. I expect the police update later today. Max Graham was sighted in the area. Have any of you heard from him?" I watched as all the councillors shook their heads. I decided to give them the benefit of the doubt, for now. "Do any of you have any questions for me?" Another unanimous shake of heads. "Then Jamie, can you please start with your update?"

"That went well," Seamus commented two hours later as he trailed behind me to my office. "Did you see the message from Jon?"

"Yes, and yes. Just for something different, why don't we meet at Evie's in half an hour, for lunch? Can you let Jon and Lara know please? I just want to check my emails." I'd a niggling feeling I needed to see something that couldn't wait. "Oh, and can you please confirm the time, date and location for the town meeting with Mikayla. I promised I'd let Izzie and Lexi know asap so they can advertise it."

Seamus side-eyed me, "You know I'm not your personal secretary, don't you?" He joked, "But seeing as you mentioned lunch, I suppose I can make an exception, this time."

As he left, I opened my council emails, which contained all the normal requests for meetings, development applications, and other emails I referred to as adverts. Emails from contractors offering their services. One email stood out, not just because it was written in upper case. The title – LEAVE TOWN NOW, was eye catching enough. The body of the email contained more of the same – LEAVE TOWN NOW OR YOU'LL REGRET IT. The sender's name was gobbledygook. My heart thumped loudly in my chest as I reread it, before sending a copy to the printer.

With my intuition telling me to take my laptop to the café, I shoved the offending email into the bag with my computer, nearly running into Seamus as I left my office. "What's the rush?" He asked, narrowly missing being hit in the shoulder with my computer bag.

I couldn't speak, the lump in my throat blocked my intention to tell my best friend about the second threatening letter of the day. I shook my head, to clear the cobwebs. "I was coming to check on the details of the meeting, on my way to the café."

Seamus took my free hand in his. "I don't believe you, but we'll discuss that later. Friday, 9am, the high school hall. Mikayla apologises if that doesn't suit, but we both know that whatever time we choose, someone will complain. People who want to attend, will."

"Thank you. I'll text those details to Izzie and Lexi, is it appropriate to ask them to mention the mayor and councillor supports the meeting and encourages participation?" I asked, my fingers tapping away on my mobile.

"I think that's a great idea! The meeting is focused on how to help the tenants of Wynyard Street after all," he replied, opening the outer door as I continued to type the message to my friends.

Chapter Twelve

A short man, dressed in three shades of green stood on the footpath barring our way. *Evie's Café* sat a few doors down from *The Magic Shop,* only a few minutes on foot from the council office. From his emerald green top hat, his lime green shirt to his dark green trousers, the leprechaun, for that's what the man reminded me of, wasn't moving out of our way.

"Excuse me sir, may we pass?" Seamus asked the gentleman, with his shiny black shoes and his walking stick.

The man, who stood not quite as tall as I did, pointed his finger at me. "You were warned. It's not too late, step down, leave town, don't follow the same path as your ancestors." He twirled himself around swinging his coattails around him and disappeared.

I blinked. "That was weird." My brain tried to figure out whether he vanished or walked quickly back into the store. I turned and strode towards the front door of the shop that promised to teach magic.

"Where do you think you're going?" Seamus asked, his hand on my arm sending tingles around my body.

"Why to see what the old man meant," I responded. "I'm sick of baseless threats, people who think they can set fire to my buildings, of everyone behaving so stupidly!" I knew I was ranting.

"Didn't sleep much last night?" My friend didn't have to read my mind to figure that out. "How about we have some food first, and I'll come in the shop with you, after lunch, on the way back to work?"

"Seems reasonable," I acknowledged, as my stomach flip flopped, though whether from hunger or anxiety I couldn't quite tell.

Lara smiled as we arrived at the door to the café at the same time. Evie's front door, made of dark wood with an opaque glass insert, contained tiny specks of colourful lights threaded through it. The door opened, just as Lara reached out to hold it open. Two thin men, both so tall they nearly had to duck as they exited, pushed past us, as they spoke to a third person on a tablet in front of them. Both men wore navy trousers and black polo shirts, with a logo too small to see, even when I squinted.

"What is it with rude people?" I exclaimed, adding for Lara's benefit, "We had an incident outside the magic shop." I mentally dislodged my crankiness, and smiled at Lara, "How's your Monday been so far?"

We lined up behind a group of older women in beige skirts and cream blouses. "The women's bowls team," Seamus whispered for my benefit.

"A little weird, if I'm honest," Lara said. "More customers than normal, have been asking for ingredients for spells, which is fine by me, but I don't normally have those types of questions. At least they knew what they were looking for and didn't expect me to provide them with the actual enchantment."

We shuffled forward a little until we were next in line to order. Behind Evie, fairies were cleaning the bench where the shiny silver coffee machine sat. "What were the spells? Did they tell you?" I wondered if there was a theme or a reason for the increased magical activity.

"Not everyone shared that information, though some were quite chatty. Love, healing, protection are the spells I remember. Is it important?" Lara spoke quietly.

"Hi everyone!" Evie beamed at us before I had the opportunity to answer Lara. "What'll it be today?"

Seamus spoke up before Lara or I had a chance, "How about chicken salads and pineapple juice, with coffee and jaffa cake for dessert, for four of us please."

Evie raised her eyebrows, "Certainly! Great choices. Go and find a table and I'll get mum to bring them out to you."

The table we liked, near the kitchen swinging door, was empty. I led the way there, sliding into the first seat. Seamus scooted in beside me. Lara chose the seat opposite me, as Jon entered the café. She waved him over to join us.

"Sorry I'm late," Jon sat beside Lara.

"We just sat down. I ordered a healthy style lunch for us all," Seamus grinned.

My spider senses tingled. I looked around the café. Apart from the women's bowls team gossiping over milkshakes, the normal businessmen, a few mothers with toddlers, I didn't see anyone I didn't expect to see. No Max, or Dean, or man in emerald green. "What is it?" Seamus asked quietly.

"I'm not sure, my intuition keeps telling me someone or something is watching me, or maybe following me, or I'm just sleep deprived," I added, seeing the looks of concern on my friend's faces.

Jon leant forward, "You've not seen anyone, or been threatened?"

I considered my options. My stubbornness encouraged me to keep the threatening notes to myself, but I knew better than to do that. The three people in front of me had my back. I pulled two pieces of paper out of my laptop bag. "I found a piece of paper under my welcome mat this morning. Then I received a threat via email. There was a weird man outside the magic shop. Seamus and I are going to pay a visit to the shop after lunch," I handed the pages to Jon.

I crossed my legs, and my arms waiting for the stern words from Seamus and the others. Luckily the kitchen door swung open, and Bessie appeared, with four plates of salad with crumbed chicken pieces.

"Bessie, thank you," I smiled, genuinely happy to see Evie's mother. She always wore such colourful dresses and aprons that matched her wide, warm, welcoming smile. Today's dress and matching apron were green, with tiny pink flowers.

Bessie smiled as she put the plates on the table, her face changing to one of sadness as she touched my arm, "I'm so sorry about the fire. I'll be back with your drinks in a minute. Enjoy your lunch," She disappeared through the swinging door.

Jon held up the papers I handed him. "Would you have told us about these if I hadn't asked?" I wasn't used to seeing such a stern look from Jon. Seamus's face was just as bad.

My gaze fell on my hands. I tucked them in my lap, hoping no one noticed they were shaking. "Yes. I knew we'd meet for lunch, which is why they're in my laptop bag, I even tucked the first one into a plastic bag, in case you could find prints on it." I held my hands up, palms out, grateful my energy had calmed. "You know me, I don't like to create a fuss."

"Hmm, well..." Jon placed the papers on the table. "These are hardly articulate, meant to scare you, I guess. We might get lucky with fingerprints. Good job with bagging it. The email, I'll get Fred on to trying to discover the sender." He looked hungrily at the plate of food in front of him. "One last thing, before we eat, there were no fingerprints or evidence at the arson scene to point specifically to a suspect."

"As we suspected," My stomach grumbled, indicating I needed to eat something. "No more interruptions, we have yummy food in front of us, let's enjoy it."

Chapter Thirteen

The door to the shop didn't budge. Seamus rapped on the glass with his knuckles. Nothing. I peered through the window, trying to see past the magic toys on show, but the heavy black curtain prevented me from seeing anything beyond the window.

A slow drumming, the sound reverberating through my body, emanated from inside. I reached for Seamus's hand as my knees buckled. "It's the drumbeat, there's something about it, we need to get away from the door." He stumbled, as we forced our feet to move away from the sound. The sound faded with each step.

My hands tingled as my skin touched Seamus's. I gently pulled him with me, step after step, until the vibration no longer thumped through our bones. By the empty shop on the corner, we could walk independently. Our hands remained tightly locked together, for the walk to the council office.

We reluctantly untangled our fingers, as Seamus opened the glass door to the foyer. "6pm, your house?" His voice was raspy, whatever we'd just experienced had spooked us both.

I nodded, not trusting myself to speak.

The sense that we were being watched stayed with me through lunch, and as we said our goodbyes. After the weird episode outside the shop, my spider senses tingled.

If I'm meant to know or remember something, help me out. I sent my message into the ether. Would my parents or grandmother hear and respond? There were too many distractions for me to focus on the unknown right now.

With no scheduled meetings for the rest of the day, my plan was to sit at my laptop, respond to emails and plan the community meeting. Grateful for the kettle I'd bought into the office, I made a black coffee, and sat at my desk, my laptop screen open showing me the council emails I'd yet to open.

In contrast to my office at the newspaper, the mayoral office furniture contained no character or warmth. When Max fled, he took everything. All the paper records, stationery, his computer, even the office chair. The big, heavy mahogany desk with the black insert on the top and the equally dark wooden row of low cupboards, the only items left in the room. I'd brought in the office chair, the kettle, a couple of mugs, and some pens, notepads, other stationery bits and bobs, deciding to use my laptop instead of bothering with a computer.

A couple of years before I returned to Spirit Town, I'd invested in a laptop with a large capacity for running several programs at once, never dreaming I'd need it to run a newspaper office and a mayoral one. It's security protocols passed the approval of the council computer geeks, who sat somewhere in the back of the building.

A few months ago, when a similar chain of events led to me taking on the newspaper office, I'd found Lexi. Her first job had been to source computers for the office. Luckily, she'd networked the newspaper computers with my laptop. I sighed, investigative journalism had changed from the days when a pen, paper, and a typewriter were the only tools I needed.

I wiggled my fingers and toes. *Focus Beth, work now, freak out later.*

Acknowledging that Max and Dean were likely deliberately working to conspire against me, helped a little. I knew from Dean and my ghostly cousin Jacob that the chain of events that led me to return home had been orchestrated by a group of people with magical powers. Jacob referred to them as a coven. I didn't understand why my stepping into the role of mayor upset a group of strangers who didn't live in the town. It was true that Max and the group now called Majestic Mirage, were keen to build on the Wynyard Street site. How did the owners of the magic shop fit into the story? I straightened my back, made some notes in my notepad. I outlined what I needed to know. Research to uncover information, a plan to move forward. Seeing my thoughts on paper calmed my thumping heart. Feeling less anxious, I drank my remaining coffee and turned to my laptop.

The first three emails were easy to answer. The enquiries from local businesses asking for the process to bid for council work. I referred them to Kim Watson, who managed business support, amongst her other portfolios. Max's past dealings favouring local businesses hadn't gone unnoticed. Ensuring transparency and accountability could be a tenuous tightrope. Our office coordinator and first point of contact with the public, Mikayla, demonstrated great people skills. Her attention to detail, and organisational abilities vital as we'd ensured all electronic records were labelled and stored correctly. She'd given the council website a makeover, making it easy to answer the next couple of enquiries, about development applications and forms.

An email titled *general business* didn't stand out, I almost missed it, having clicked on it earlier without reading it. The body of the letter, although not in capitals, contained another barely veiled threat – *You'll regret sitting in that chair madam mayor.* It sounded like Max. He'd spoken to me in that tone while he sat in this office. He didn't scare me then, being more bluff than muscle. The email had the same tone, of a school yard bully trying to bluster and blame someone else for their indiscretions.

What did concern me about our former mayor was his ability to bully our inexperienced youth who were only just learning about their powers to carry out crimes. I printed the email and added it to the copies I'd taken of the other threatening notes. I emailed it, and the earlier threat to Jon, as I'd promised to do.

Rather than standing and going for a walk, as I felt like doing, I made myself check and respond to all the remaining emails. That meant reading a couple of reports which took longer than I thought. I kept losing concentration but forced myself to complete the task at hand. Finally happy I'd done enough mayoral work, I stood, stretching my arms out above my head, and headed for the front office.

"Beth, I'm sorry about the fire," Mikayla looked up from her computer. Her short hair dyed a vibrant red, matched her dark green dress, making her look a little elfish. She handed me a framed drawing of the shops in Wynyard Street. "I hope it's okay that I drew this for you," she added, her voice barely above a whisper. Her artistic ability was amazing. After only seeing a person or place once she could draw it in amazingly accurate detail. I'd encouraged her to pursue her dream of art school, though I'd be sad to lose her, she had an terrific way of making all council visitor feel immediately at ease.

I blinked as droplets trickled down my cheek, wondering when I'd run out of tears. "It's beautiful Mikayla, thank you so much." I wanted to hug her but was aware of the workplace and our roles.

"I've printed off the details of the town meeting for you, and all the questions we've received so far. I included the questions from before..." Mikalya hesitated, her cheeks reddening, "When there was talk of inappropriate behaviour."

"Don't be embarrassed on my account," I said, a little too harshly. I softened my voice as I continued, "People will talk and expect the worst, it comes with the job. Thank you, I do need to know all the questions, what people are saying and thinking. I know my words won't necessarily be believed. Actions speak louder."

"This is why we need you as mayor. You're not afraid to speak up. I was there that first time, when they vandalised the park. You spoke to the crowd, to assure them it would be okay." Mikayla stated with a fire in her voice.

"Gosh, thanks, I just don't like it when bullies try to brow beat others and pull the wool over their eyes. Speaking of which have you heard from or seen Max?" I remembered the reason for visiting the front desk.

Mikayla sat up a little straighter. "No, but I've heard rumours he's back. Did a lawyer really get him out of prison?"

"Apparently. Please keep an eye out for him. Not that he's dangerous, but he isn't trustworthy. Speaking of which, can you contact each council member and ask if they'd be happy with new locks being fitted. We don't want Max accessing the building. Please tell them I asked you to follow it up for me. If they all agree, please contact a locksmith to come out as soon as possible." I couldn't believe I hadn't thought of it earlier.

"I'll do it straight away. What about the other staff? Cleaners and other tradesmen with keys to the building, did you want me to ask them, or just tell them after we change the locks?" Mikayla jumped up out of her seat, her voice filled with excitement, "I know! Why don't we change to electronic locks where we have a four-digit code to enter the building?"

I thought about her suggestion. "It sounds like a good idea. If Max has anyone who'd be likely to lend him a key, it wouldn't matter whether it was an actual key or an electronic code. Can you ring the councillor first and check they agree with the proposal, get the locksmith out, then ring the others who need to know. You choose the four digits. Just ring to tell people, don't write it down not even in a text or email." I looked at the clock above her desk, realising I'd just given her a big task in the middle of the afternoon. "I'm sorry, do you have time to get on to this now? If you've other priorities, you could start first thing in the morning."

"Now is fine, I can multi-task," she grinned.

As I turned to head back to my office, the front door opened, and Agnes walked in. "We need to talk."

Chapter Fourteen

I sat across from Agnes, knowing if I offered her tea or coffee she'd refuse. She drank dandelion tea, and other teas that I'd not yet remembered to keep on hand. I knew better than to start with small talk, knowing my mentor would get straight to the point.

"Your office is bugged," she pointed to the front corner of my desk, the tray on which the kettle sat, and the windowsill. Sure enough, as I followed her directions, I found three tiny microphones, no bigger than my fingernail and nearly as flat. I poured water from the kettle into my mug and popped the three devices into the liquid.

"Do you remember any of the spells Beryl taught you?" Agnes continued. I shook my head. "Well, then pay attention." I stared at Agnes's hands as she weaved the story of Grandma sharing her magic with me. As my mentor shared my past, playing in front of me as if I were watching a movie, I found myself murmuring the words of the spells as Grandma taught me. Agnes folded her hands in her lap. "You're a quick study, which I never doubted. You just had to be ready, willing to learn, to remember. That spell of protection, cast it as you leave your office, and as you arrive home. It'll stop Max, Dean, and others with less than pure motives from entering the space."

I recovered my senses enough to ask, "The new shop, that pretends to sell magic toys, what can you tell me about it?"

Agnes stared over the rim of her glasses, into my eyes. She slid her hands into the long loose sleeves of her black dress. "Every time you ask someone, the answer will change, as can be the case with what is commonly referred to as *black* magic. You've already met Dean, and you know of the coven he *belongs* to. Hiding in plain sight, changing their names, their appearances, those in that shop have hidden agendas. Opening their back room to 'teach magic' is just one of the ways they're asserting their influence."

I nodded agreement, "Dean made it clear to me that he worked with some powerful magicians who weren't happy with me as mayor, for reasons I haven't quite figured out."

"Your heritage, which Beryl wanted to share with you, but Madge and Lyle wouldn't agree, is key. Speaking of which..." Agnes raised an eyebrow.

"Not yet," I didn't want to say too much, in case they were still able to hear us, which made me sound paranoid, or crazy.

My mentor understood. With a curt nod she stood. "It's your path, to discover the cause and the solution. I can guide you, but it must be your discovery. Start with the spells." As she shook my hand, she palmed me a small piece of paper, no bigger in size than a matchbox. I walked her to the door and watched as she floated along the footpath until she faded into nothing.

Mikayla followed me into my office, "The councillors agree to the change of locks. Jason, the locksmith can be here at 7am tomorrow. I'll be here to let him in, collect the code and other details, and let everyone else in as they arrive." She handed me a folder. "You left the meeting details behind, when Mrs Moggle arrived."

I took the folder, placing it in my laptop bag. "Thank you, Mikayla, I appreciate you getting onto this task so quickly. I'm heading home via the newspaper office. I'll be here by seven tomorrow as well. I'm contactable by phone or mobile, if you need me," I glanced at my watch, "Although it's nearly five, I hope you're heading home soon."

"Just as soon as I check my emails, and lock the front door," she smiled. "I'll see you tomorrow.

Did Agnes mean I was to cast the spell outside my office or outside the council chambers? Would it make a difference? I closed my eyes, to find that memory of Grandma. *As long as your intent is pure, the spell will work.*

"Okay then Grandma," I whispered, "*By the power of three protect this building and all who serve, Keep it safe from those who seek to do wrong, We stay on the right path, aligned and true, Magic deep inside and all around, So mote it be.*"

A warmth spread from my toes, through my body, to the very top of my head. A giddiness wave passed through me, leaving as quickly as it came. I held onto the door frame for a second, getting my bearings. *Did that work? Let's hope so.*

Agnes hadn't mentioned the newspaper office, but I decided I may as well protect it too. As I entered through the front door, I heard Lexi on the phone in the kitchen, so I headed straight to my office and repeated the enchantment. This time I was prepared for the wave, planting my feet firmly on the ground as it hit.

"How was your day?" I asked as Lexi popped her head in the doorway a few seconds later. "We've had such a great day!" Lexi said, reluctantly handing my kitten to me. Spark licked my face, before snuggling into the crook of my arm. "I've sent you an email, with some questions about the town meeting. Izzie and I are sharing information, we agreed I'd brief you, if that's okay?"

"Perfectly okay with me, thanks Lexi. Can you make sure all the doors and windows are locked tight, with Max around, I want to make sure we are safe. What do you think about key code locks?" I wondered if I should get Jason to change the locks here after he finished at the council.

Lexi's eyes darted up to the right, indicated she was considering my question. "I'm not a fan to be honest. You, Seamus and I are the only people with keys. A bigger building, like the council, I can see merit, but not here."

"That's a very good point, I tend to agree." I tried to hide a yawn.

"If you don't mind me saying so, you need to go home and try to sleep," Lexi, stroked Spark's ginger fur. "This guy will sleep too. We've worn each other out chasing balls of string."

"Thanks Lexi, I don't know what I'd do without you. I'll be at my other office early tomorrow. Spark should be fine at home," I cuddled my kitten, despite him wriggling, trying to jump out of my arms.

"Aww, if you're sure. It's never a problem having him here," Lexi said, patting me on the arm, as I left the office, closing the front door behind me.

My short drive home was uneventful. Placing my shopping from earlier in the day on the verandah, before I unlocked the door, I again chanted the spell Grandma taught me. The energy, stronger than before started in my left hand, moving along my body, and out through my right. Spark paused his interrogation of the verandah, tiled his head quizzically, then continued to sniff around the furniture. "Good boy Spark, I knew you were clever, I didn't even have to tell you what I needed." The door lightly vibrated under my touch as I unlocked the front door, which I took as a sign that my incantation worked.

My feet dragged as I walked from room to room, checking nothing had changed in the last eight plus hours. "Did I leave my desk like this?" I asked Spark as we entered the dining room. The two piles of paper on my desk were askew – not hugely but enough that I doubted I'd done it. "No windows are open, nothing in here could've knocked the piles." Not that there was anything of importance in the documents, mostly research I'd done into Max, the Majestic Mirage corporation, and some background on Spirit Town, including what little information I could find about my parents' and grandmother's deaths. I opened the grey metal filing cabinet and tucked the papers into the top drawer. I locked the cabinet and pocketed the key. A yawn escaped my lips, the type of yawn where you can't help but make noise as you suck in the air and expel it with force.

My palm tingled as I ran my hand in a half circle in front of me. An image of a spritely figure in black came into view, fading as quickly as it did. I'd a feeling I'd seen the figure before but couldn't place him. "Come of Spark, let's check Buddy." I rummaged in the bags I'd dumped in the kitchen a few minutes earlier and pulled out an apple. Spark tiptoed at my heels as I opened the back door, breathing a sigh of relief as my sheep's familiar face greeted me at the bottom of the steps. "Hey Buddy, here's a snack for you. I don't suppose you can tell me who it was who's been sneaking around? It didn't look like Max, maybe Dean, or another of Max's henchmen?" Buddy nose tickled my palm as he nudged around, hoping for more food. "Later Buddy, I'll bring you a carrot in a while."

"I need cold hard facts," I muttered, more to myself than Spark, as I boiled the kettle, making a mug of peppermint tea. "No more guessing, or magic, though if my family want to send me answers from beyond the grave, that'd be good." I emptied the contents of my laptop bag onto the table. Needing order, I organised the items.

My laptop, the threatening notes, and the folder Mikayla prepared in one pile on the table. I sat my notebook and pen on top. I laid my keys, wallet, and mobile on the kitchen bench. That left the key Agnes handed me, and a chunk of clear quartz crystal. "I know I didn't put this here," I held the crystal point down to Spark, he sniffed it, but didn't appear too concerned. "Is it one of Grandma's?" I didn't expect my familiar to answer me. Intuition like a gentle touch on the bridge of my nose, prompted me to close my eyes. I saw Grandma, holding a clear quartz crystal, telling five-year-old me that if I ever needed answers, to use the crystal point.

Chapter Fifteen

"What did you do with the door?" Seamus asked, dragging two full shopping bags into the kitchen. The smell of Chinese food wafted into my nostrils, breaking my daydream, where Grandma and I were walking through the garden, talking about the magical properties of herbs.

"Mmm, that smells amazing. You have enough here for an army, are Lara and Jon joining us?" I placed a pile of plates and cutlery on the kitchen table, relocating the laptop and papers to my bag, hanging it on my chair.

"Door?" Seamus raised an eyebrow, "They'll be along in a minute. We have Chinese for dinner, ice cream and cake for dessert, and pineapple juice with lemonade for something different."

"Thanks, I'm glad you organised this, I owe you one." I placed the tub of chocolate chip ice cream in the freezer, shivering as the cold air tickled my fingers. "The door, yes, I've placed a protection spell on the house." Before I could say any more, we heard a knock at the front door. I opened it, letting Jon and Lara in. "Thank you both for coming here for dinner."

"We should be thanking you, and Seamus for arranging it," Lara replied with a smile.

"All I've done is supply the chairs, table, plates, and cutlery. It's been too big of a day to do anything else," I sank into the chair closest to where I stood. "Please make yourselves at home. Thanks, Seamus, for the effort of getting this together for us."

While the others scooped rice and other foods onto their plates, I remembered I hadn't fed my kitten. I dropped a handful of dried food into Spark's dish, filled up his water bowl and set the kettle to boil. Returning to the table with glasses for the juice and lemonade, I eased back onto my chair. Noting my tiredness, but choosing not to comment, Seamus poured four tall glasses of the mix, placing one at each person's plate.

"I hope the rest of your day was quieter than the morning," Lara commented as I scooped some rice and chicken onto my plate.

I placed the spoons back in their plastic containers. "There was a weird experience on the way back to work, and I received a visit from Agnes. Another threatening email, and I'm certain someone broke in here and rifled through my papers. On the plus side, I remembered a protection spell Grandma taught me. The house and both workspaces are now protected, and I found a crystal point, I think it was Grandma's and that it'll somehow help me find the answers."

Jon placed his fork on his plate and drank half the liquid from his glass in one gulp. "I've proof that Max is in town, living in an apartment locally, though we've not yet been able to find or question him. Dean is proving just as difficult to pin down. He lives overseas, in Germany, and Italy, for most of the year, and appears to have more than one name. It's terribly messy."

I sighed. "Why don't we try not to think about any of this tonight. Let's eat our dinner and talk about other things. For instance, Lara, how's your shop going? You said more people were coming through, which is awesome." My taste buds exploded with flavour as I ate my dinner. Not a big eater normally, maybe my body needed the energy, to fight through the stress, and whatever magic forces kept trying to attack.

Lara smiled, "It's been a good day. I asked Agnes if she'd run some short workshops, in store, on the magical properties of herbs. She agreed, which is so exciting. What's wrong?" she asked seeing the look of surprise on my face.

"I had a vision earlier, or maybe a memory, of being with my grandma, she was teaching me the magical properties of the herbs." I smiled at the feeling of love and belonging it evoked. "I think it's great you and Agnes are working together to support our community.

Seamus reached for the fried rice. "Does anyone mind if I have seconds?" He asked, "Don't worry, I'll still have room for dessert."

Jon patted his stomach. "You go for it. My tummy's full and I'm saving room for cake later," he paused, "Can I ask a question? I know we were changing the subject, but I'm curious about something."

"Go for it," Seamus responded, his plate piled high with the remaining hot food.

"You guys know I moved here earlier in the year, so I haven't learnt everything there is to know about the town and residents." Seamus and I nodded. Jon continued, "Some people have magic, all different sorts, some people don't, and for the most part that works well. People leave town, and there's no consequence, and people move here, and settle in, whether they possess magic or not. Are there ever any consequences, or bad feelings between those with magic and others? Is it always amicable?"

Seamus swallowed the mouthful of food, pausing before scooping up another. "There's not normally any fall out from people moving here or away, most people tend to get along, the same as anywhere else. You experienced what happened with Max. That sort of behaviour is the exception around here. You know Agnes and the others provide space for those with gifts to practice their skills. The town doesn't keep a register of people with magical abilities," he pointed his thumb at me, "Although I know Beth's thought about it. How it would work though, would be a nightmare."

I squeezed my hands tightly together, as I spoke. "I do think it would be useful, but I agree it'd be a nightmare to keep the register accurate. What you don't know is, my parents, and my grandmother before them, were some kind of leaders in the magical community, and had the authority to banish people who used their magic to hurt others. I've only recently become aware of this." I looked to Seamus for confirmation that I'd worded it properly. recently.

"Yes," Seamus spoke quietly, reaching over to still my hands. The warmth of his skin on mine sent pleasant shivers down my back. "Beth's parents, and her grandmother before that were leaders in the community and did have the power to exile people like Max, who used their magic for evil, to coin a phrase. Since Madge and Lyle passed away, Agnes has taken on a leadership role, more of a mentor, and neither she, nor anyone else has been exiling people. It was deemed too dangerous." I nodded, as he searched my face before he continued the story. "It appears Beth's parents, and grandmother may have been killed because of their actions."

Looks of shock, horror, and pity flashed across Lara and Jon's face. Their hands joined on the table, as they sought to comfort each other. "I think the reason Dean tried to attack me, my role as mayor, and destroy the shops in part was to keep me from taking on the role vacated by my parents. It wouldn't surprise me if he was somehow connected to Majestic Mirage, or Max."

"Max isn't magical in any way, he is just a horrible, selfish, obnoxious man," Seamus added.

Lara raised her hand, "That's horrible about your family, and scary," her free hand found mine and squeezed it. "I have a question too, Beth you've discovered more of your own powers, since moving home and coming to terms with your magic. Do you know of other people who move here, and discover latent powers? Do most of the others in town know about and use their powers from birth or discover them later?"

"Great questions, I think most residents with special abilities learn about them from their parents, and around the age of fifteen we generally start experiencing and experimenting with them. I don't know anyone who's moved here. Except the two of you," I gathered our empty plates, standing to take them to the kitchen sink.

Seamus looked up at me, "I think that's the point. Lara, Jon, are you both experiencing abilities you didn't know about?" I dropped the plates on the bench and sat back down as both Lara and Jon nodded. Seamus's ability to read people never ceased to amaze me.

Lara's cheeks reddened as she spoke, "I told you I was adopted and never knew my real family, that I moved here on a whim, and I was sick of the hustle and bustle of the city." I leant in as Lara spoke, keen to hear what ability she had. "It started slowly, customers would walk into the shop, and I'd know why they were there. I thought my guesses were flukes. Now, I'll be walking along the street, or in the café, for example and I'll know which people will be coming into my shop, and why."

"Wow, a great gift for someone who owns a health food shop. I'm so happy for you," I squeezed her hand, "er, I mean, if you are happy that you have the ability to read people."

"I am, mostly, now that I am used to it, initially it was a little scary." Lara looked at Jon.

"You too?" I asked.

"Yes. It appears I can tell how people feel. I think it's called being an empath? It's so draining, but I'm getting used to it, slowly. Not just emotions, I seem to know if a person is good or not...I mean Max has a dark cloud around him, Seamus doesn't...am I making any sense?" The policeman stopped talking, frowning at his own jumbled thoughts.

"To me, what you said, makes perfect sense." Seamus collected the empty Chinese containers, swapping them for a delicious looking caramel mud cake. "Did you know you had magical heritage?"

Jon shaved head moved from side to side. "Not at all. Both my parents are lawyers. They work in criminal law in the city. They'd not heard of Spirit Town and can't understand why I felt drawn to move here, when the vacancy came up. I'm not sure myself, it just seemed like a sensible career progression, being a promotion."

I pulled the container of ice cream out of the freezer, and added bowls and spoons to the table, and a knife, so we could cut the cake. "It can't be coincidence, that the four of us became friends when we found ourselves working on solving the mystery of the missing gates, before the festival," I mused aloud. "Have your abilities changed recently?" I asked my oldest friend.

"I could always read you, what you were thinking and feeling, and occasionally other people. It happens more frequently now. Anyone I walk past, their thoughts will pop into my head." He raised an eyebrow, "I'm training myself to switch that off, you can imagine some of the things I *hear.* I can still pull anything apart and put it back together without any directions. I don't need maps to find my way around, and no, not just because I've lived here my whole life. It's like my awareness is growing, which sounds odd when I say it out loud."

We silently pondered the revelations we'd all shared, as we ate our cake and ice cream. It couldn't just be our abilities that were growing. Were others in town also finding an increase in their powers? What did that mean for Spirit Town? Could we all live in harmony? How do we keep people with less than pure intent from moving here, or moving away and creating havoc? Did we need a gatekeeper, someone to keep those with magical ability honest?

Chapter Sixteen

As I scooped the last skerrick of ice cream and cake from my bowl, Spark's front paws tapped my calf. I reached to pick him up, bringing him onto my lap. "Hello little guy, were you feeling left out?" I moved my chair back from the table, in case he was angling for some dessert.

Lara bundled the bowls together taking them to the sink. "Do you mind if I leave, once I wash up, it's late and I've had an idea for how to re-organise the shop, I'd like to get started early tomorrow morning."

I stood, with Spark in my arms. "I'll wash up later, I appreciate you, all of you, coming for dinner and sharing your stories with me. I'll try to come into the shop tomorrow, I keep meaning to, but I get side-tracked."

"Anything you need, just tell me and I'll drop it by the office," Lara smiled.

"Thanks, and I may take you up on that, but I still want to see your shop for myself," I smiled back, popping Spark back on the ground, so I could take the glasses to the sink.

Jon pulled his mobile out of his pocket, "I'm heading off as well, if you don't mind, I've got to check in with Fred before I get some sleep. Thanks for dinner and the company."

"Anytime," Seamus and I said in unison. The sound of laughter echoed through the hallway as we walked to the door.

After promising to catch up with Lara and Jon the following day, Seamus shut and locked the door. "No argument, I'm taking Grandma's bed, I know you set the protection spell, but I'll feel better knowing you aren't alone. That, whatever it was, outside the magic shop today freaked me out more than I like to admit."

I stared into my oldest friend's face, knowing he'd reluctantly agreed to be *just friends* so we could focus on our respective businesses and our obligations on council. Without overthinking it, I enveloped him in the tightest bear hug I could manage. "Thank you," I whispered, "I'd like that. It was freaky, whatever happened there, it's been playing on my mind, how we protect ourselves from that type of magic." Eventually, I let my arms drop away from Seamus, turning so he couldn't see me blush, I led us back into the kitchen. "Would you like more cake with your coffee?"

"After I check all the doors and windows," Seamus grabbed the carrot I'd left on the bench before he opened the back door. I heard him greet Buddy as I ran the water for the kettle. I started the washing up, quickly setting the plates, bowls and cutlery to dry. Finding a clean cloth in the cupboard under the sink, I wiped the sink, the benchtops, even the table where we'd all eaten, full of an energy I didn't know I had in me, this late in the evening. Nervous energy. Positive nervous energy.

I heard the rattling of window locks as I set up my laptop. This time I emptied the contents of my bag neatly onto the table. "The house is locked up and secure, geez, we're not sitting up and working all night, are we?" Seamus joined me at my adhoc desk "Don't you have an entire room seconded as an office now?"

I carried two mugs of hot choc, a packet of which I'd found in the cupboard, still in date, and a plate of cake to the table. "Not all night," I grinned, blushing again, "I just want to check something." I breathed a sigh of relief, as no more threatening emails sat in any of my email in-boxes.

Seamus picked up the key Agnes had given me. "Did you find whatever this opens?"

I shut my laptop, transferring it to the kitchen bench and plugging it into the charger. I did the same with my mobile phone. "No, I didn't fancy going into Grandma's room alone, though I'd planned to have a look tonight. Not that I didn't enjoy the dinner and the company, thank you. Lara and Jon are good friends, it was a great distraction."

"They are good people," He held out his hand, "Let's look for the journal together," he suggested quietly.

We both felt the connection, that warm tingling sensation, as we held hands and walked through the door to Grandma's room. It was more than the connection with Seamus, the bond I shared with Grandma was still as strong now and thirty years ago. "Last time we were here we found the series of ledgers she kept, listing all the unusual occurrences in Spirit Town while she sat on the magic council."

"I remember, it blew me away that she kept records, until then I thought it was only your parents, who kept an informal list of local events. I've learnt so much since then. Why don't you start there in the wardrobe with those ledgers, and I'll tackle the scary shelves." I couldn't help giggling at the memory of a much younger Seamus, too sacred to sneak into Grandma's room with me, because of the rows of potion bottles, and her vast stone collection.

"Hey, no fair, I know they're just crystals and bottles of herbs – now." He play-punched my arm, "but yes, I'm happy to check the wardrobe."

The dresser, an antique, solid, painted white, the curved top carved with squiggles and symbols sat along one wall of the room. The higher shelves were packed with books about herbs, plants, crystals, and natural remedies. Rows of bottles of common and uncommon herbs came next, *lavender, peppermint, rosemary, mugwort, wormwood,* I ran my fingers along each book spine, and each jar, my spirit aching to reach any residue of Grandma still lurking after thirty years. Did I imagine it, or did the sensation of her touch grow stronger as I moved through the shelves? The stones, or crystals, sat in individual wooden square boxes, which joined together to create a display case.

Seamus's muffled voice broke into my thoughts, "How are you going over there?" His head popped out around the side of one of the wardrobe doors.

"Spider senses are tingling," I replied, "And you?"

He re-entered the room, closing the wardrobe, "It's not in there," he stated. "Oh my..." I turned, to see what caught his attention. The brass handle on the little door, underneath where my hand was hovering glowed brightly. Not a trick of the light, the metal, though not hot to touch, lit up the closer my hand got to it. Seamus came and knelt next to me, so close I had to focus, to concentrate on the glowing metal in front of me, instead of the close proximity of my best mate.

I expected the metal to be warm under my fingers, but it wasn't. Neither was it cold, rather room temperature, which I didn't expect. I turned the handle and opened the cupboard door. The space inside, little bigger than a shoe box, held a box and a pile of colourful fabric. As I unfolded the fabric, I gasped. The handsewn patchwork squares formed a beautiful, long, flowing gown. The term *dress* didn't seem to describe it fully. "It's beautiful," I whispered. I laid the gown on the end of the bed.

Seamus lifted the box, placing it on the bed next to the dress. He took the lid off, revealing a thick red leather-bound book. "The secret journal," he breathed. We both stared at the book, no bigger than a regular sized notebook, its worn red leather cover, tied with a large red strip of material, had my grandma's name stamped on it. A small brass lock lay under the ribbon. I looked from the journal to my friend and back to the journal. "It's okay," he said quietly. "It's a lot to take in, you don't have to pick it up tonight."

Before I could answer, the lights flickered, and we were plunged into darkness.

Chapter Seventeen

I took Seamus's hand, leading him by feel to my bedside table, which contained a flashlight with fresh batteries. "Ouch!" Seamus muttered, "It's only my ankle, keep going." I suppressed a smile, as my fingers knocked over a pile of books next to my bedside, as they searched for the portable light.

I clicked the button, and a faint ray of light shone in front of us. "I don't suppose you know where the fuse box is?"

"Why would I know where it is? It's your house," Seamus pointed out.

I shone the light towards Seamus, careful not to shine it in his face. "You've spent more time here, in the last twenty years than I have, helping my parents, I figured you might know."

"As it happens, I do." I heard the grin on his face, though in the torchlight, it was difficult to tell. He pulled me towards the front door, "It's on the wall of the house, at the end of the verandah."

"At least the power is out across town, it not targeted at our house." I pointed out as we opened the front door. The lack of streetlights didn't help us see what we were doing. "Shame the moon is tucked behind a cloud."

"It's over here, though if the whole town is in darkness, it's pointless to check the fuse box." Seamus held my hand, moving it so the torch light shone on the metal box attached to the wall. "It doesn't look like it's been tampered with."

I sat on one of the wicker chairs where I'd sat with Grandma, my parents, and Seamus, the blue and white handmade cushions made the bumpy wicker more comfortable. My eyes slowly adjusted to the dark. Seamus walked down the steps, looked up and down the street, and returned to where I sat. My kitten's rough tongue tickled my foot, as he joined us. "Where have you been little guy?" He nuzzled my fingers as I stroked his fur.

Seamus's phone beeped. "Jon says the whole town lost power, it should be back up and running in ten minutes."

"I wonder if it's teenagers, playing with their powers again?" It had happened a few months ago. When high school kids accidentally opened a portal into the past. I'd fallen through that portal myself a couple of times, seeing Grandma as a younger woman.

"Jon thinks it's more likely a straight forward act of vandalism. Wires were cut at a couple of key locations around town. I'm hoping it doesn't lead to thefts, though last time the thefts were very specific." Seamus checked his phone again.

I drummed my fingers on the table, "Stationery and vitamins was a very specific shopping list." I agreed. "Did we ever work out what was going on with that?"

"We got a little distracted with Dean, your cousin Jacob who can materialise at a second's notice, and you being accused, and cleared of wrongdoing," I heard the sarcasm in my friend's voice.

I reached over and touched Seamus's hand. "It'll be okay, we can work this out together. Why would someone turn off the power to the whole town? What are they trying to achieve?"

"Maybe to break in to somewhere, to steal something, or damage something," he suggested. "Does the power fuel anything unusual?"

"You're asking me?" I said incredulously, "You mean like anything magic, but again, you're asking me? Should we look through Grandma's ledgers? Once the lights are back on, it'd be tough going by torchlight."

A distant wail of a siren reached our ears. "That doesn't sound positive," Seamus commented. "Do we make a cuppa with that camp stove? You put it back under the sink after we used it, the last time the power went out."

"I did, then I moved it, to the bottom of the pantry cupboard. I found a couple of big candles and another torch – they're in a plastic tub next to it. A packet of matches too, before you ask," I added reading his mind for once.

Seamus read the text as his mobile beeped. Even with the lack of light I saw by the colour of his face that something was wrong.

"What is it?"

"The sirens we heard were from an ambulance. Agnes has been in an accident. She'll be okay but has to stay in hospital overnight at least. The community hall where the weekly meetings are held has been ransacked. She tried to stop the intruders and got a hit on the head for her bravery.

I jumped to me feet, my heart sinking to my toes, "Did Jon give any other details? When can we visit? Will she be okay?"

Seamus stood, wrapping his arms around me. "She's a strong old bird, she'll be fine. Just bumps and bruises Jon said. She needs her rest tonight, We'll visit her before work, I'm sure they'll let the mayor in outside of visiting hours. Rather than coffee, let's sneak some more ice cream, before bed, by candlelight. I mean, we can't do anything about Agnes or the blackout now, I know you're worried. I'm just trying to distract you," his voice faded off, sounding unsure of himself.

Thankful my friend couldn't see me blush, I nodded. "That sounds nice, I don't think I could sleep anyway. Did Jon say if anything was stolen at the church?" The magical community held meetings at an old, abandoned church every Thursday evening. A place where those with powers felt safe and supported, were able to ask questions, and learn about their craft. Agnes led the group, there were rules, and most people agreed to them. Initially on my return to Spirit Town, I rallied against the teaching of magic skills, back when I still feared mine. Having come to terms with who I was, I now strongly supported everything Agnes did for the magic in our community.

I wiggled my toes as my familiar's paw tickled my foot. "Spark wants us to follow him." I knew from experience that he'd keep patting me until I obliged and checked out what he wanted me to see. Holding hands, I shone the torch in front of my kitten and shadowed him into Grandma's room. In one jump he landed on the bed, on top of the beautiful gown.

I gasped, immediately seeing the problem. The bright light stung my eyes as the power returned. I blinked, until the light spot dissipated. "What the?" I leant against Seamus as I saw the extent of the damage. The box containing Grandma's journal no longer sat on the bed, and her wardrobe doors were thrown wide open revealing empty shelves where her town ledgers previously lined the wall. "How on earth did someone come in here and take it all, with us outside?"

Seamus pointed to the open window. "I know I locked that earlier." I heard the anger in his voice. Not someone who irritated easily, when he did, I wouldn't want to be on the receiving end of his rage. "Max couldn't have pulled this off by himself, though if he's working with Dean, it'd be possible. Our ex-mayor probably knew your family kept ledgers."

My energy bubbled just below the surface. "I set a protection spell as soon as I got home, how did it not work?" As I spoke, I saw Agnes pointing to the microphones hiding in my office earlier in the day. Without thinking of what I was doing, I waved my arm in front of me, "Reveal yourself!" My voice sounded firmer, with more force and authority than normal. "Well, that was weird, I don't know what I expected…"

"I do," Seamus strode over to the bedhead, removing a tiny mic from where it was hidden. He moved from room to room, pulling out similar bugs, while I made us coffees and bowls of ice cream.

Chapter Eighteen

Spark followed me as I opened the back door, "Are you okay out here?" I patted the top of Buddy's head, "It's not food time yet, I just wanted to make sure nothing was disturbed out here." It didn't look like anyone had trudged through the garden. It was a little overgrown and in need of some attention. So where did the intruder go after climbing out of the window? How did they get to her window, for that matter?

Seamus had the bugs soaking in a glass of water. "I think we have an answer to that question," he pointed to a piece of paper on the table, the back of one of the threatening emails that we'd been looking at earlier.

"Jacob," I read the words scrawled across the page. My cousin, a man I didn't know existed until a couple of weeks ago, communicated via words on paper.

Dean and Max have help. You can stop them. If you choose correctly.

"What do you mean?" I asked, knowing it'd be fifty-fifty whether he'd respond. Jacob belonged to the same coven as Dean. He could appear and disappear at will. In my sleep, I'd eavesdropped on conversations between him and Dean. I wasn't entirely convinced Jacob was on my side, but his handwritten notes helped me win against Dean, last time.

I can't tell you – you must choose

"Go away Jacob, you're either helping, or you're not. I've no time for games." I hoped exasperation might encourage him. When no writing appeared after a few seconds, I bundled up the papers, tucking them into the manilla folder. "Ice cream, and coffee," I indicated for Seamus to join me at the table. "If Jacob can come and go, Dean, and the rest of that coven likely can as well. So that explains *how* they got in and out of Grandma's room. The *why* is also easy. To stop me from figuring out what's going on. They don't want me to know what their end game is. They also want to discredit me, make me give up, and leave town, which I won't do."

I'd scraped the last of the ice cream from my bowl, as I heard a gentle tap at the front door. "That's an improvement, at least someone is asking to come in," I couldn't help the sarcasm, as Seamus opened the door.

"Do you mind if I come in? I know it's late," Jon sounded tired, and apologetic.

"We're just having a cuppa, if you'd like coffee, or maybe peppermint tea?" I refilled the kettle.

"Peppermint tea sounds good," the policeman sat next to Seamus. "I thought it would be easier to update you in person."

"That sounds ominous," I placed a mug of tea on the table.

"According to Agnes, the intruders took all the documentation stored in the community hall. The records of magical incidents, going back years, a little like the ledgers. The files kept track of the training, initials only, residents weren't named, to protect their privacy. She didn't know if anything else was missing, but Mike is going to check and let me know." Mike helped Agnes with the gifted community, focusing on the youth, helping them adjust to their abilities. Jon sipped his tea, using his free hand to extricate his notebook from his shirt pocket. "Since the power went out, we've been called to the town swimming pool, which is now full of lime cordial. The park, where giant snowmen are melting in the new rose garden. The town gates, which appear to have been welded shut...the calls keep coming. Nothing too dangerous, more mischievous. As if young kids have been given the keys to the toy shop and are driving all the robots and remote-control cars along the roads, which god forbid I hope doesn't happen." He clasped his hand over his mouth, horrified at the image he'd conjured.

"Someone, probably Dean, broke in, while the power was out, and we were sitting outside. Stole all Grandma's ledgers, and her secret journal, which we'd just discovered." I dragged my notebook out from under the manilla folder and scribbled a note to ask Agnes about the enchantment.

Jon's mobile beeped, "I don't know whether to call for additional resources, we're not dealing with a crime wave. It's more like misdirection, magic gone haywire, which I'm not looking forward to telling my superiors about." He held up his mobile phone, "Some of our streets have turned into slippery dips, or roller coaster rails, causing quite a concern to people who were on the road in their cars."

"Oh, my goodness. Okay, mayor hat on now, we need to let people know, not to worry, but to watch out for strange occurrences. I'll text Izzie and Lexi, we'll put some information out through the paper and the radio, also through social media." I tapped a text, sending it to both Lexi and Izzie.

Seamus put his hand on my arm, "Slow down, you don't have to do it all yourself."

I smiled at him, "I know that. I was merely making a head start. It's late and unless all the crazy goes away before sunrise, there'll be a lot to do. How's Agnes?" I glanced at Jon.

He looked from me to Seamus and back, with a wry smile. "She's tough, shaken, but already asking when she can go home. I left the doctor to tell her she had to stay at least until tomorrow morning," Jon read the latest message to come in on his mobile. "Do you mind if I go? I've got to help Fred with crowd control at some of the sites."

"Of course. Do you need some help?" Seamus asked, with a sideways glance at me.

"I'll be fine here; they've already taken what they wanted. I'll lock up after you go. Come back later if you like. Your key will work in the lock." I hoped I sounded braver than I felt.

"I'd appreciate it mate," Jon turned to me, "If you're sure."

"I'm sure," My brain whirled, thinking of all the things I had to do, as mayor and as Beth, magic person who seemed to be in the middle of it all.

Seamus looked conflicted. "I'll be back, no arguments, lock up after me."

As directed, I followed my friends to the door, sliding the lock in place as they left. I didn't bother to try for sleep, whether the result of too much coffee or sugar, my energy focused on what I could do to help.

I drafted a letter to Lexi and Izzie, confirming my text, asking them to let the community know to watch for unusual occurrences. I added a post on the local social media sites, urging anyone to be cautious when out on our local roads.

My vision blurred, as in front of me I saw Grandma as a younger woman, in the old church, talking to three young men. Another image of the same room, but with my parents in animated discussion with two older males. Were they the same men, or related to the younger three? My intuition told me both images were of people being banished from Spirit Town.

Trust, believe, embrace your power. The ghostly whispers were so close, so real, I spun around, expecting to see my parents standing behind me. My senses tingled; my electrical energy stronger than before as little sparks of light escaped my fingers before I could stop them. Thankfully the tiny rays of light vanished as soon as they left my body.

Grandma knew the old ways. Knowledge passed through the maternal side of the family for generations, until my parents decided I wasn't to learn what they took for granted. Dad's ancestry was a mystery to me. As I was growing up the stories they shared were of both being only children, and that on my mother's side, only females were born, going back generations. My trip through the portal into times past, revealed that to be untrue. My great grandmother had a brother.

I sighed. Secrets and mysteries, my life was getting more complicated by the day. When I closed my eyes, I could hear Grandma's voice as she told me the meanings of herbs, crystals, and words from books. My memories were real.

In the middle of Grandma's room, I sat cross legged, Spark stood in the space between my knees. I assumed my abilities were like Grandma's and Mum's, though I'd never properly thought about it before. "Any information here, was removed by Dean, or one of his henchmen," I told Spark, who'd given up on me going to bed, and had curled up in my lap. "So, it's all about my intuition, and logic. I can do this." Spark purred his agreement.

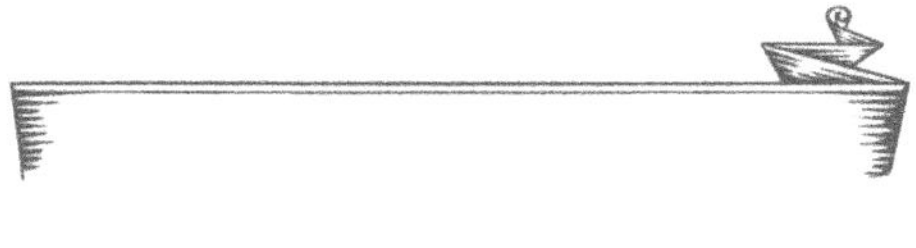

Chapter Nineteen

I filled my mug with tap water, drank it, refilled it, and drank again. The digital clock on my laptop told me the time was 1am. I yawned, not willing to go to bed. I found a chocolate bar, and some strawberries in the fridge. "Am I trying too hard?" I asked Spark. "Maybe I'll just do some work, try to stop thinking about the other stuff."

Sitting on the floor in Grandma's room I'd conjured up images of Grandma using elemental magic. Creating the garden out of the earth, using air, water, fire and spirit. Could I create like her? I'd never noticed either of my parents using magic in that way. Not sure what I expected, I wasn't suddenly filled with an innate knowledge of what to do.

Compelled by my frustration, I focused on what was within my control. "The town meeting later in the week, should I move it up?" Spark patted my hand with his paw, a message I took to be to leave the meeting set for Friday. "You're right Spark, no good going into a meeting unprepared, I can always talk on the radio or just post updates on social media as and when we need it." I opened my laptop, pulling up an internet search bar. "What was it Seamus called Ralph's magic?" I asked my kitten. He looked into my eyes. "That's right," I typed elemental magic into my search bar.

The ability to manipulate the elements – earth, air, fire, water, and spirit.

"If Grandma possessed elemental magic, she'd have the earth element. She could grow any type of plant. Mum could cook, sew, and make anything from simple ingredients. "I don't know what type of magic that is. I wish you'd met my parents Spark, and Grandma. I know they lied to me, kept the truth from me. I remember they had such a way with people, they could make anyone feel at ease. Though I guess not to those who were exiled." I felt my anxiety, or lack of sleep, and frustration build up inside me. I inhaled, and held my breath for the count of five, slowly exhaling, and repeated the exercise a couple of times.

The front door opened. "Are you planning on sleeping at all?" Seamus looked as exhausted as I felt.

"Probably not tonight," I admitted. "Although I might have a nap after lunch tomorrow."

"How about we at least lie down for a while, neither of us will be any good to the town if we nod off in the middle of a meeting," Seamus gently closed my laptop.

I yawned. He made sense. My bed was queen size, more than enough room for us both to rest. "Okay, but only if you let me set the alarm for six and tell me all about what's going on in town."

"Deal. Come on little guy," he picked the kitten up off my lap, holding him in his arms. I picked up my mobile and turned off the kitchen light as I led the way to my room. "I remember the last time we had a sleepover; we were seventeen and swotting for our final exams."

"You insisted on sleeping on the floor, even though the bed's big enough for us both." I grinned at the memory.

"I thought I was being a gentleman," he said, "though if you want to sleep on the floor tonight, go right ahead."

"I think we can both lie down on my bed, three of us if you count Spark," I couldn't help giggling. Spending time with Seamus had that effect on me. I felt like a teenager again. We lay on either side of my bed, with Spark snuggled up in the space between us. I yawned, as Seamus started to tell me the scene he and Jon had been met with.

The next thing I knew, incessant beeping jarred me out of a dream where a giant gingerbread house sat where the council building should have been. My eyes flew open as I moved and kicked Seamus's shin.

"That's a great way to wake up a person," Seamus rubbed his leg.

"Would coffee help? And I'm going to regret saying it, but I'm sure there's a piece of cake as well," I swung my legs over the side of the bed.

"Now you're talking!" Seamus lifted Spark onto the floor and checked his phone. "No messages from Jon, or anyone else, hopefully that means there's been no more dramas overnight."

I doubted it but wasn't keen on voicing my concerns. After all, anything could happen. "Coffee, and cake, first, then we check on everything else. I promised Mikayla I'd help her with the locksmith at 7am this morning, and I also want to visit Agnes. Do you have a busy morning?"

Seamus, cut two generous slices of cake. "A couple of committee meetings, nothing I can't change if I have to."

I took an apple and a carrot out of the fridge, filled Spark's bowl with some diced chicken, and headed to the back door. "I'll just feed Buddy," I opened the door, "Er, maybe you should come see this." The leaves on the trees were shimmering yellows, blues, reds, and other shades as well. "It looks like someone's plugged fairy lights into the trees..." Mum spent hours on the garden. Natives lined the perimeter, just in from the fence, and larger trees in the middle of the garden created shade for the other plants. Fences kept vegetables and herbs protected from Buddy. Similar lights in the backyards visible over the fence, assured me it wasn't just my backyard. "Poor Jon and Fred are probably still out answering calls," I shook my head. I joined Buddy at the foot of the steps, handing him the carrot.

"Last night, there were so many calls, about noises, shadowy figures, water in backyard swimming pools turning to cordial, fires spontaneously starting in fireplaces, flowers growing in the middle of the road, other streets turning to sand." Seamus patted Buddy, as I held out the apple for him. "It's like all the teens learning their skills all at once. Surely it will calm down soon."

Buddy nuzzled our hands, enjoying the company. Spark sniffed around behind us. "If Max and Dean are behind this, it feels like a distraction, a way of keeping us all occupied looking in one direction while they are up to something obvious, in plain sight." The fire, a blackout, theft of my grandmother's journal and ledgers, and now magic going haywire around the town. Whatever the cause, I dragged my feet up the steps, knowing we'd both have a busy day ahead.

Chapter Twenty

I braced myself, pleased I decided to hop into Seamus's ute. The short trip to work was bumpy as the road appeared to be temporarily made of giant pieces of popcorn and breakfast cereal moving on a conveyor belt. "Who benefits from making it this difficult to move around Spirit Town?" I wondered aloud as he did his best to avoid the pops and bangs of the random bits of food exploding under the vehicle.

"I'm not sure if anyone chose to do this. I get the distinct impression that people's powers are misfiring, or malfunctioning, and that they are powerless to stop it. Worse than when we were teenagers. It's like the magic is just oozing out at the worst moments." We both indistinctively ducked, as a medium dog sized dragon swooped the ute. "The question is, how do we stop it?"

"Maybe Agnes will have an idea, if anyone could do anything about this chaos it would be her." I mused, as we pulled into the carpark at the back of the council chambers. The insects partying in my stomach calmed a little, as the building didn't seem to have suffered from any enchantments.

Seamus opened my door for me, as I juggled my laptop bag and Spark. I'd decided not to leave him at home after all. His little warm body comforting as he snuggled into mine. "After we see Mikayla, and drop Spark with Lexi, we'll pop into see Agnes. Then maybe we could check Evie's is okay?" he added hopefully.

I smiled despite the goings on. "Feeding you is a priority," I agreed. "I'm grateful for your help, and company." I prayed my cheeks wouldn't decide to flush as red as a tomato, as they often did.

Mikayla met us at the door. "Beth, Seamus, hi, Jason is working on the front entrance first, then he'll update the side entry, and this one. I imagine you'll both be busy, I mean, what's with the weird stuff? Did you know the gates have disappeared again? Firstly, they were stuck together, now disappeared. Marshmallows are growing on trees; others have leaves glowing brightly..." she shook her head. "The radio reports, and social media is going crazy."

I put a reassuring hand on her arm, Spark nudged Mikayla's hand with his little nose, purring loudly. "When people ring or email and ask about the goings on, or what we are doing, please tell them that Seamus, the others on council, and I are looking into it and hope to have a resolution soon."

Seamus raised his eyebrow, "Maybe you should tell the others that's our position too."

I handed Spark to Mikayla. She snuggled her face in his fur. I grabbed my phone and tapped on the keypad as fast as my fingers allowed. "Just sending a text now, to all of you, telling everyone I'd recommend this to be our position and arranging a meeting for 9:30am this morning. This is our priority."

Mikayla held Spark up in front of her face. "He's adorable," she gushed. "Apologies for asking, but should the other council, the magic one, be looking into what's happening? I don't mean to offend anyone."

Seamus checked his phone. "They are, I spoke to Mike last night. He's contacting the local youth to make sure it's not directly related to their powers. Jon and Fred are working non-stop on it as well. Agnes, Mrs Moggle, one of the key members of that council was attacked last night. We're going to visit her in hospital this morning."

"Oh, I'm so sorry, I didn't know," Mikayla handed Spark back to me, "You can leave him here with me if you need to. I'm sure he'll be no trouble."

"Thank you, but Lexi looks after him during the day, if I don't leave him at home. Thank you for coordinating the lock change, we'll be back by 9:30am." As we hopped into the ute for the short trip to the newspaper office, I added for Seamus's benefit, "We should be able to squeeze in a quick breakfast beforehand."

He clutched at his stomach, with mock hunger pains, "Thank you so much madam mayor." I grinned, if I hadn't been holding my familiar, I would've punched his shoulder.

Lexi opened the door as we pulled up in front of the office. "Thank goodness you guys are okay, I was worried, especially after what happened to Agnes," she enveloped us in a group hug, squashing us together. As we separated, Spark had mysteriously moved into her arms. "Hey Spark, it's you and me today. Before you go, what do you need from me?"

I smiled, grateful that I could trust her to get the information out for me. "Can you please coordinate with Izzie, wording something like, not to panic, mayor and councillors are working with police and others in the community to resolve the issues. Update as soon as possible, refer to the town meeting on Friday. Can you also upload a similar post on social media please."

"Will do. Don't worry about a thing," she said, as the shrill ring of the office landline reached us. "I'd better answer that," she swung around so fast her pigtails whipped around tickling Spark's tail.

Before we could climb into the ute, a group of elves, dressed in green overalls ran past, carrying buckets and spades. "They are a lot more people out early in the morning than normal," Seamus observed, as a procession of cars drove slowly past, rounding the corner towards the park. Finding a gap in traffic, we pulled out from the curb and followed the cars. In the small fountain at the beginning of the path that wove through the park, sat the elves and half a dozen small children. We leant forward to get a closer look. "I think, the fountain is full of lollipops and small toys. What's impressive is the children seem to be taking turns." More parents and children joined the line that had formed, waiting for the children to have a turn in the fountain.

The drive to the hospital didn't provide any additional surprises, apart from the two dog sized dragons that flew past, and the group of fairies picking cupcakes out of a gum tree. Cars driving slowly, looking for any more unusual occurrences, obeyed the road rules. "At least this road, seems to be normal, and no buildings have turned into giant gingerbread houses either," I observed, crossing my fingers lest I jinx the remainder of the journey.

Chapter Twenty-One

Nurse Doreen, a lady I'd known most of my life, who'd patched up cuts and grazes at school, dispensed medicines, cold packs and icy poles as the school nurse, manned the nurses station. "Beth, Seamus, you're here to see Agnes. Hopefully you can talk some sense into her. She wants to go home, now. Just walk out of here like she's not nearly seventy and hadn't been knocked over by an intruder less than twenty-four hours ago. At least get her to stay until the doc does his rounds." Her stylish short grey hair tucked into a blue fabric hat that matched her scrubs. According to my calculations Doreen and Agnes were roughly the same age.

"We'll see what we can do," I knew once Agnes set her mind to something, it'd be difficult to dissuade her.

"A lot like you," Seamus whispered with a grin as we followed Doreen to the first door on the left. Hospital décor could do with a makeover. Agnes's room, like the corridor, and the reception area, was light grey and cream, the walls and the plastic furniture. Angular, sparse, boring. Not an issue within my control though maybe I could raise it at a future council meeting.

Agnes sat on the bed, fully dressed in a black dress, her hair wound on the top of her head in a bun, glasses on her nose, her bare feet dangling over the edge of the bed. "Beth, Seamus, thank you for coming. They won't let me have my boots, probably worried I'll walk home, as if not having footwear would deter me. Now you're here, you'll drive me."

"Why don't you wait and talk to the doc, when he gives you the all clear, you ring me and I'll drive you wherever you want to go," Seamus suggested, sitting on the bed next to our old English teacher.

Agnes side eyed Seamus, looking him up and down, with a harrumph. "What about you?" she turned to me, "Do you agree with young Quinn?"

I slid into the hard plastic chair beside the bed. "As it happens, I do. I also have questions. Do you know who it was, and what they were looking for at the community hall? To me, it feels like Max and Dean. Could they be trying to steal towns records, and create havoc, misdirecting us to look in one direction while they set something in motion? My other question is how do we fix what's going on? Roads turning to jelly, lights and food growing on trees, snowmen in the park, lollies in the fountain..."

My mentor crossed her hands in her lap. I thought she may be going to show me a scene from my past, weaving a story as she'd done before. Instead, she said firmly, "You've come along faster than I dared hope for. It is Max and Dean, trying to confuse everyone, so they can takeover Spirit Town, while we aren't looking. By distracting you and I, and others like us, who'll stand up to them. Only one person can put this right, stop the crazy and return our town to normal."

"It's not me, I couldn't even set that protection spell properly. Dean, or someone working for him broke in and stole all Grandma's ledgers and her secret journal, before I got to read it." My heart pounded in my chest, I'd never forgive myself for letting her words get stolen, for not making a point of knowing more about the town and my family.

"Rot and nonsense. You don't need ledgers and journals to right this wrong," she pointed to my hands as they tingled, my energy activated by my emotions, again. "Your energy, your emotions, use them to clear the magic chaos. You tend to hide from your strongest emotions. Instead of running away, use them, as part of your strength." Agnes gave me that look, that sent prickles down my spine. I swear she could see into my soul; past all the walls I'd built to protect myself. "Don't be so sure your protection spell didn't work. Have you checked the items have disappeared, or are they maybe still there but invisible to human eyes?"

Seamus and I looked at each other, eyes wide. "I didn't think of that," he admitted. "So, Beth's spell worked, and the books hid themselves from the intruders?" Agnes nodded. "How does Beth 'fix' the current issues?" It feels like the magic of our gifted residents is being amplified, oh I see, her powers will also be amplified." Agnes raised her eyebrows as Seamus worked out what might have happened.

My brow furrowed. "I'm not sure it's as easy as it sounds. Won't Dean just re-cast his spell, creating more chaos, making it a cat and mouse, chase my tail scenario?"

"Not if you believe in yourself and your abilities," Agnes tone took me back to high school. "Just because you walked away, and your parents didn't talk about your magical heritage, doesn't mean you don't have the ability. You come from one of the most powerful families. The form that power takes, is up to you. Stop using your past as an excuse not to live the life you were meant to."

I knew from the way she looked at me, that Agnes meant every word of it. One question remained. How do I make myself believe in my own strength and ability? "Can you at least tell me what my main power is? What I remember from growing up is that Grandma and Mum possessed different strengths. I feel like mine is unlike either. My sense is that my strength is elemental, though I only just learnt what that means." I tried to get the words right in my head. "I feel connected to the town, to the earth, the plants, and the people, even though I don't know many of them by name. I'm fiercely protective, even passionate."

"Or stubborn," Seamus interrupted with a grin.

"You are all those things, and if I'm not mistaken, you just answered your own question." Agnes swung her legs back onto the bed.

"I might stay here to talk to the doc after all." She pointed at Seamus, "You will come and get me when I call you."

"I will," he replied earnestly.

Agnes reached for the book on the table beside her bed, indicating we were dismissed. "I'm glad she's in such good spirits," I murmured as we left her room, passing Doreen as she approached Agnies room with a breakfast tray.

"Did you see the toast, cereal, fruit, yoghurt, and juice?" Seamus whispered.

I tucked my arm in his, "I'm taking you to breakfast, for being the best friend ever." Agnes' words had charged my energy. I felt I could do anything, well almost anything. Saving the town seemed less daunting than a relationship with my best friend.

"You can do it," Seamus read my thoughts, blushing, "You can achieve anything you put your mind to, after breakfast," he added, opening the passenger side of the ute for me.

Chapter Twenty-Two

I glanced at my watch. We drove past the park, where the crowd around the fountain had grown considerably in the last half an hour. Their arms full of cupcakes and biscuits, plucked off trees full of similar baked goods. The road ahead glowed orange, and shiny. "I'm not going to risk that, it looks slippery," Seamus turned left off the main street, parking behind our office building, in one of the few remaining empty spaces.

I stepped gingerly onto the footpath. The rubbery black surface was a little tricky to navigate. My foot bounced up each time I stepped on it. "It's like walking on a trampoline. How did they come up with this stuff? Especially if Agnes is right and they didn't steal the ledgers after all."

"Just sheer bloody mindedness I reckon, they just want to cause chaos." Seamus changed his pace, so his boots trod lightly, saving himself from flying into the air. "Hold my hand, please, I don't want to have to climb onto a roof to save you," I could tell my friend was annoyed.

"Let's get you whatever food you want for breakfast. We need all our wits about us for the day ahead." I opened the door to Evie's.

"You may regret that, I'm starving," Seamus cheered up at the thought of food. "How about a bacon and egg burger, some hash browns, toast, juice, coffee, and whatever you want," he asked hopefully, sounding like a kid in a lolly shop. "I see Jon talking to Mike, I want to hear the latest news, if you don't mind."

"I don't mind at all," I joined the back of the line. "I'll join you as soon as I order." I strained my ears, paying attention to the voices of those around me. My sense of hearing fine-tuned from years of investigative journalism, though eaves dropping didn't come naturally. Being new to the role of mayor, I tended to wait for residents to approach me. Maybe it was time to change my approach.

Two women in the line in front of me, similar in age to me, both with hair tied back in short ponytails, in navy slacks and white shirts. "Can you believe what's going on? I know many of us have unusual abilities, but it's awfully odd that it's all happening at once," the taller of the two women commented.

"It's like when we were at high school," the other woman agreed, "Maybe it's a whole group of teenagers playing around at once." Before the other woman could answer, it was their turn to order. I turned my attention to the group of people waiting for their takeaway orders. A couple of men in overalls, and an older woman with a green dress, stood silently, staring at their mobiles, waiting for their order to be filled. Their auras appeared muted, maybe they were still waking up, or worried about the weird events.

"Hi Beth, what'll it be?" Evie smiled as I approached the counter. Her colourful hair, green today, tied in pigtails, with two fairies behind her cleaning the coffee counter, no wait, I looked closer, they were making the coffee! I rattled off Seamus's order, choosing something different for myself. Evie laughed at my distraction, fascinated by watching small fairies making coffee. "Have you only just figured out how clever my helpers are?"

"I'm lost for words, but thank you, for making our breakfast," I recovered some semblance of decorum as I approached the table where Jon and Seamus were seated. "Mike's not still here?"

"He wanted to be at school, to be available for any teens who were upset about what's happening in town." Jon rubbed his forehead wearily. "I've given Seamus an update, I have to head off myself soon, but I'll try to touch base with you later this morning." He covered his mouth as a yawn escaped his lips.

"Maybe you should duck home and have a nap?" I suggested.

"Maybe," he waved as he exited the café, I knew he'd not be napping until the perpetrators of the chaos had been identified and apprehended.

As I slid into the seat next to Seamus, Bessie bustled over with two big plates of food. She placed in front of Seamus everything he asked for, as well as extra pieces of bacon and eggs. My plate contained a fresh fruit salad of berries, bananas and mango, with a hash brown. "I hope you like your food; I made these especially for the both of you," she beamed.

"Mind?" I could kiss you!" Seamus jumped up and hugged Evie's mum.

"This looks delicious, much better than anything I could've put together," I added.

Seamus tilted his head towards me and winked, "She's right Bessie, Beth here can't even make toast without burning it."

Bessie laughed, "I think you've exaggerating, but it's good for business, unless you start cooking at home yourself." She started humming to herself as she floated back to the kitchen. At least it looked like she floated, her yellow, green, pink and blue floral dress covered her feet, giving the illusion of gliding. Evie arrived at the table, placing a tray with two glasses of juice and two large takeaway mugs on the table. "I figured you'd be busy, so we made your coffee 'to-go.'"

"Thanks Evie, we do have a few meetings this morning," I smiled at our hostess.

"We may be back for lunch," Seamus murmured, stopping his fork before it reached his mouth. Evie and I shared a look, rolling our eyes, before she headed back to the counter.

While Seamus made short work of his full plate, I savoured the sweet taste of the fruit on mine. The bananas were perfect, just ripe enough, and the sweetness of the mango with the raspberries made my taste buds do a happy dance. The less sweet blackberries, and tiny blue-

berries blended perfectly with the banana. Just the energy kick I needed.

"Jon and Fred are run off their feet, even with the volunteers who
are willing to help monitor the crazy events. No one's been able to re-
verse any of the magic. All they can do is cordon off the worse affected
areas. I don't mean to make a point of it, but when were you thinking
of trying to fix it?" Seamus spoke quietly. I got the impression he was
trying not to upset me.

I waited until I'd finished the last piece of mango, before I spoke,
"After we meet with the other councillors. I want to make sure Grandma's ledgers and journal are at home as Agnes suggested. Then I'll do
my best to right the situation. Will you stay with me while I try?" I
cleared my throat, aware my voice sounded funny.

"I wouldn't be anywhere else," his voice as quiet as mine.

Less than half an hour later, our plates were clean, our bellies were
pleasantly full. I picked up my takeaway mug. "Let's get to the council
chambers. I want to check social media on the way, to see what is being
reported on, where the hot spots are."

The floor shook as we walked out into the street. Every couple
of seconds there was a jolt, as if a giant was running along the road,
though none were visible. With each thump, the road, the buildings
shook, and windows rattled. All thoughts of social media and emails
vanished.

Chapter Twenty-Three

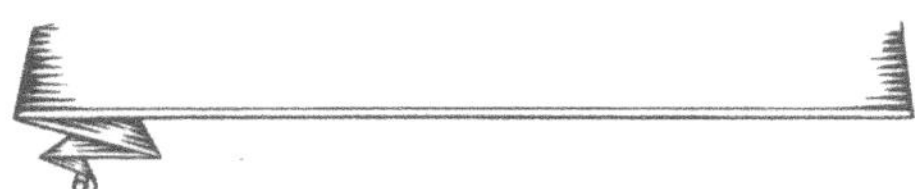

Panicked residents ran around the street, ducking into shops, only to be shooed out as equally panicked shopkeepers tried to leave their shops. "There are giants in the park!" A teenager on a bike sped past, pedalling as fast as he could. "Another one at the high school." Behind him, other teens cycling and running out of the park followed him.

"What do we do? Where do we go?" A couple of older women, in jeans and blue shirts tripped on the loose pavers on the road, as they looked for a safe place to hide.

Sirens started in the distance as the giant footsteps continued to shake everything. Seamus and I looked at each other. "I can't wait until after the meeting, can I? I can't even wait until I make sure those books are safe at home." Seamus stared at me, the tears welling in his eyes, were the answer I feared. I watched as terrified horses and cattle ran along the road, cars swerving to avoid hitting them. "It's okay." I tried to reassure him though my voice was barely above a whisper, "You need to go help Jon and the others, to try and keep everyone safe."

"Where will you be?" My oldest friend asked, the colour draining from his face.

I didn't know myself until I opened my mouth to respond, "In the middle of the park, in the new garden George created for the festival earlier this year." The place where I'd spoken up, inadvertently challenging Max's leadership. Appalled at his lack of commitment to the towns folk, I spoke, to bring calm to a community scared by senseless acts of vandalism. In a way, this was the same, but on a much larger scale. I hugged Seamus tightly, willing that it not be the last time we saw each other. He returned the hug, the same emotions coursing through our veins, joining together, providing that extra strength for the task that lay ahead. Without looking back, lest I faltered, I strode purposefully to the middle of the park, in the middle of Spirit Town.

It was only when I stopped walking, that I noticed a good portion of the people from the main street had followed me, looking at me expectantly as the noise of oversized footsteps echoed a few streets away. In the direction of the main street screeching tyres, screams, and angry mooing added to the eeriness. I pulled myself up to my full one hundred and sixty-five centimetres, swaying my arms back and forth to gather my energy, and my thoughts. "I know you're scared, this chaos is terrifying. I want you to know it's not any of our residents who are causing it." A murmur of surprise rippled through the crowd. "Max Graham has returned and is working with a man named Dean Collier. Dean has strong magic powers, more than most of us. They are affiliated with the Castle Home project, now renamed Majestic Mirage. It appears they are misdirecting magic, creating havoc to distract us, so they can do something underhanded..." I didn't know this for certain, except that my gut, that feeling deep in the pit of my being knew it to be true.

"What are you going to do about it, madam mayor?" I strained my eyes to see who called out, but the wind whipped up a willy-willy of dust and sparkling particles, obscuring my view.

"My heritage is one of magic power, though I chose to run and hide from it for years. I'm now willing to face that strength I inherited from my parents, my grandmother, and my other ancestors." I held my arms out straight in front of me. A gust of wind emanated from my hands, clearing a path that had been cluttered with dust, dirt, leaves and branches. "Don't be scared, but maybe move to one side," I told the people standing close enough to hear me.

Rather than yell to be heard above the commotion, I chose my quiet voice. That one reserved for people who annoyed me.

"I call my elemental magic to me, I call the power and strength of my ancestors to join with me, to banish the chaos from Spirit Town. Earth, Air, Water, Fire, Spirit all – calm the earth, the waters, the very core of nature. Return the peace to our town, stop those who'd seek to harm our home. Through the power in me and around me I ask this, knowing it will be done. So mote it be."

Not sure what I expected, the silence that followed my words surprised me. The dust vanished, there was no more rattling, and from where I stood, I saw no evidence of unusual magic activity. The flora in the park seemed to be back to normal. The fountain contained only water. I held my hands by my side, concentrating on slowing my breathing.

Before I could gather my thoughts enough to speak, the crowd gathered in the park, slowly moved away. I heard them speaking, quietly amongst themselves, no words that stood out to me. "Thank you," a little girl in school uniform tugged on my jacket. Her blue checked skirt and pale blue shirt looked worn. I smiled at her, as her mother led her away, to where a group of parents with similar aged children stood. Each of the parents smiled at me as they took their children's hands, and headed in the direction of the school.

An older man, dressed in khaki overalls waved as he joined me, "Miss Beth!" I'm so glad I found you," George the council gardener shook my hand enthusiastically. An old friend of my fathers, his dark wavy hair and moustache moved as he spoke. "I wanted to say how sorry I am to hear about the shops in Wynyard Street," he shook his head emphatically. "Also, I've designed a plan for the spring and summer flowers, in addition to the bulbs, and wanted to pass it by you before I order anything."

"I trust your knowledge and skill with plants, you have my approval to go ahead," I stopped, seeing the smile leave his face, and added "but please send me your plans, I'd love to see them, I may have questions, and one or two suggestions myself." George's wide grin confirmed I'd said the right thing. "I look forward to seeing your plans. Now if you'll excuse me, I want to check to see if things have gotten back to normal around here." George bowed, as he moved back to the garden bed brimming with azaleas. He pulled a large pair of cutters from the pocket of his tan coloured denim overalls.

With no one else looking like they were trying to speak with me, I headed back towards the main street. I scanned the trees in the park, and found no trace of glowing leaves, cupcakes, marshmallows or other unusual objects. The water under the fountain sparkled in the sunlight. An older lady ran her fingers through the liquid. "It's just water," she told her friend with a walking frame.

The main street noise, or lack of it, gave me reason to be cautiously optimistic as I walked the short block, hoping to find Seamus. People gathered, their voices the only noises to be heard, that and distant traffic. No sounds of animals in distress, no giant footsteps shaking the footpath. I exhaled a cautious sigh of relief, although Seamus wasn't in sight. I sent a text – *headed to the council office, see you there.* I tapped my finger on my mobile as I quickened my pace, expecting an answer straight away. My mobile beeped. Mikayla wanted to know if I'd be there for the 9:30am meeting. *Be there in five* I responded, deciding not to worry about Seamus, he could take care of himself.

The other four councillors were seated around the table, choosing treats from a large tray of lamingtons on the table. "Thank you," I whispered to Mikayla, nodding to the cakes. "If you hear from Seamus, can you please tell him we are in the conference room." I refused to give into my anxiety building up because of Seamus's absence. Still, I found my toes clenching themselves in my black shoes as I joined my work colleagues at the table. Mikayla passed a mug of coffee and a bottle of water across the table to me. I smiled gratefully, took a long swig of my water, and addressed the room.

"Thank you for re-arranging your morning schedule to meet with me. I'm not sure where Seamus is, but I expect he's helping Jon and

Fred, or maybe Mike." I may have been imagining it, but it felt like my fellow councillors had changed their opinion of me, or my role, or both. I no longer felt I had to prove myself with every word and action. "Max Graham and Dean Collier caused the drama we've witnessed over the last few days. Agnes Moggle reminded me of my heritage, and it appears my magic may be a match to Dean's, even though I don't yet fully understand my power." I made eye contact with each person. "There's strength in community and in remembering we're here to serve the residents of Spirit Town." My brain was spinning. "I may have managed to avert a catastrophe, but I'm aware I don't have all the answers. You've all lived here longer than I, I'd like to hear your views, ideas, comments, questions. How can we reassure the residents that we have this under control..." My fingers itched to check my phone for messages from Seamus, my common sense told me not to worry.

Glen had been a council member for a few years. I remembered him from school. Over six feet tall, skinny, with sandy coloured hair, he'd been a star basketballer for a while. "Beth, I apologise that I doubted your commitment and ability to step into the role of mayor. I'm embarrassed to admit, I temporarily forgot that you volunteered for the role. Any of us could have chosen to step into the role, but we didn't."

Jamie slid a manilla folder towards me. "Here are the updated plans for the agricultural college. We've been given an anonymous donation, which would allow the college to offer a wider range of courses, opening up spaces for more students." He sat back in his chair, "Now, I'm second guessing where the money originated from, and I wonder if we should go back to the original plans, schedule and timeline."

"I think it would be pertinent to stick to the original plans. We need to be extra vigilant with all offers of money. Kim, are you willing to assess each donation, tracing it to the true source?" Kim nodded her agreement. "I'm not saying we make any drastic changes to our schedules. Key projects still go ahead, we just add a layer of rigour around accountability." The others murmured their agreement. "I'm also keen for us to have a united position regards the strange goings on. If we are asked, I propose we say that as a council, we're working with the police and looking into the cause of the issues, aiming to resolve it...words to that effect."

"Should we work with the newspaper office and radio station to promote that same message? We could post on social media as well." Jamie proffered.

"Exactly my thinking. Are you comfortable with me touching base with Lexi, and Izzie? I don't want it to look like a conflict of interest." I was sincere, I didn't care who liaised with Lexi and Izzie, as long as the message remained consistent.

"You've proven yourself, we trust you, now, and apologise for not doing so before," Jamie looked around as the others all nodded their agreement. "It makes sense for you to be the main contact with the media."

The rest of the meeting continued uneventfully. Then I received a message from Seamus.

Chapter Twenty-Four

Can you come to Evie's please? Something in the tone of the text sounded strained. Pleased to hear from Seamus, that he wanted to meet at the café, I didn't over think it.

Give me ten minutes. The meeting wrapped up, I locked my laptop in my office and ignored the butterflies partying in my stomach.

I held my breath, but all seemed quiet in the short walk from the office to the café. Should I be worried it was too quiet?

Lara fell onto step beside me, "I hear you've been busy," she linked her arm through mine as we opened the café door.

Seamus sat at a booth with Jon, Fred and Mike. All four men were of similar ages, two in police uniform, the other two in denim jeans and deep blue shirts. All four waved as we entered.

Lara and I recognised the occupants of the table on the opposite side of the room immediately. Max and Dean, as bold as brass, at a booth with two other men. Mugs of what looked like coffee and plates of hamburgers and chips sat in front of them. The lunch crowd were too pre-occupied with their small children and their laptops respectively to pay either table any attention. I glanced at the front counter, where Evie stood glaring at Max and his cronies.

Lara gently steered me to Seamus's table. I sensed the little sparks of electricity vying to leave my fingers. On cue a fairy flitted past and with a wave of her wand and a wink she calmed my agitated energy. "You did it!" The smile on Seamus's face told me he hadn't doubted it for a moment. "I stumbled upon those two, trying to diffuse your energy.

Jon and I distracted them until you completed your spell. We followed them to the community church, then back to the café. They knew we were following them. Their goons joined them here."

"We won't be tailing them all day," Jon moved along the bench seat, making room for Lara. I took the last chair, between Mike and Seamus. "But now they know we're serious about keeping them from causing any more damage. Fred will be driving by their accommodation at irregular intervals, mainly to annoy them."

Mike passed a plate with garlic bread to Lara, who took a piece and passed it on to me. "Agnes is home, thanks to Seamus, who picked her up after the doc told her she was stronger and healthier than a person half her age. A few of us are taking turns staying with her, despite her protests." He poured two glasses of ginger beer, passing one each to Lara and me. "The high school students are coping well with the magic chaos. We're running extra classes to give them a chance to practice their powers. The more competent and confident they become, the less repercussions in the community."

I sipped the bubbly cold liquid, allowing it to soothe my throat, its flavour reminding me of Sunday afternoons on the verandah with my parents. "You've thought of everything," I admired the energy of the four men. "Thank you."

"It's a team effort," Mike commented, uncomfortable with the praise.

"Can I help?" Lara asked. "I'm at the shop most of the day, but there must be something I can do."

"I'm sure Agnes would love it if you called in and spent some time with her," Mike suggested. "I apologise for having to eat and run, but I want to visit Agnes before the end of school. After school I'm teaching a group of sixteen-year-olds how to control their energy." He nodded to where Dean and Max were deep in conversation with two thickset men, dressed in black. "Let me know if you need a hand keeping those two on their toes," he grinned.

As I watched Mike leave the café, my eyes were drawn to the other patrons. A couple of parents shared ice creams with their children in the kid's corner. The one remaining patron seated at the free Wi-Fi bench sat hunched over, reading his laptop screen. A couple of old dears sat nursing coffee and cakes. "How quickly life gets back to normal," I commented, "Which is a good thing. Have you got anything you can charge Dean and Max with?" I asked Jon.

"We need evidence, which at the moment we don't have," Fred looked to his colleague for confirmation.

"He's right, we need someone to tell us they've witnessed Max or Dean at the site of one of the incidents, evidence of them getting their hand dirty, so to speak. We're still investigating, so maybe we'll get lucky," Jon confirmed.

The owner of the café glided over to our table, the wheels on the bottom of her shoes giving the impression of fluid movement. "Can I get you guys anything else?" she asked. "I've some chocolate chip muffins, or mini cheesecakes."

"Very tempting," Lara smiled, "But I'd better get back to the shop. Thanks, though Evie."

"Ditto," Jon said as both policemen stood. "Lunch was amazing, as usual, thanks Evie."

Lara tapped my shoulder, "I'll call you later."

"Raincheck? The cakes sound tempting, and I'm sure our friend here will be ravenous later," I chuckled.

Evie smiled, "I'll save you a couple, in case you come back."

"You did good," Seamus said quietly as we walked the short distance back to the office.

I felt eyes on us, though when I turned, I saw no evidence of anyone stalking us. We crossed the road to avoid walking past the shop that sold magic paraphernalia. "Are we any closer to identifying the owners?"

"That's the one piece of information that keeps alluding us, for now," he admitted.

"If only there were more hours in the day." I sighed.

Chapter Twenty-Five

A brand-new keypad sat on the outer door of the office. Seamus scrolled through his mobile, tapping a four-digit combination onto the electronic lock, a shiny new silver keypad not much bigger than my mobile. "Only four numbers, I'll have a chance of remembering that." I grinned. I'd agreed with Mikayla in the end, that a text message was easier, otherwise, she'd keep receiving calls asking for the code for the door.

Mikayla handed us a folder each, "Before you get too comfortable, I've printed you off a series of emails I've received throughout the day. Questions, and concerns, that sort of thing. Not just about the meeting on Friday, although we've received many offers of assistance for the tenants of Wynyard Street,"

"Thanks Mikayla, do we have any meetings this afternoon?" Seamus enquired.

"Not that I know of," she ran her finger down her computer screen where the council calendar was displayed. "The others are all in their respective offices, if you want to check with them. I'll email you if anything else comes in." A pile of hand drawn images of kittens sat on the reception desk. The shades created by the pencil strokes, the depth of the features, reminded me of Spark. Mikayla noticed my interest. "I nearly forgot, I drew some sketches of your kitten." She handed the pages to me, "Would you like to choose a couple?"

"That would be awesome, thanks so much, I know I've said it before, but you're talented. I'll bring the sketches back before I go home."

"Come on madam mayor, let Mikayla get some work done," Seamus gently steered me towards the corridor that led to our offices. Ordinary white paint, vanilla is the term that came to mind, with paintings donated by local artists lining the walls. A couple of caramel coloured leather sofas sat against the wall. One near the door to reception, the other near my door. A matching sofa sat in one corner of the reception area. Darker brown wooden occasional tables accompanied each sofa.

I held my hand over my mouth as a yawned escaped. "Not going home to lie down," I shook my head, sensing Seamus's question. "I want to catch up on my reading." Lying down did sound tempting, "But maybe an early night tonight."

"After dinner?"

"Yes, pending no more disasters," I giggled, tiredness lowering the guard I held as my shield. Or maybe it was the closeness to my oldest friend that made me behave like a giddy teenager. I found myself smiling as I watched Seamus exit my office, thinking of spending time with him later in the day.

With a black coffee in front of me I read through the papers from the file Mikayla provided, the information Lexi handed me the previous day about Friday's meeting, and once I was certain I'd assimilated the information, I opened my laptop. A dozen emails sat in my mayoral inbox. I picked the low hanging fruit, responding to the simple requests first. Being mayor wasn't exactly panning out the way I'd imagined. I found myself wondering how boring what it would be like in a town without magic?

Emails responded to, I stretched my arms above my head I moved around expelling my energy. A blinking light alerted me as a new email arrived in my inbox. Entitled *Watch Your Back*. I printed the email, without bothering to read it. Whether from Dean or Max, I didn't much care at this point. A second email, from Mikayla included a list of all the pledges of support for Jan and the others. I printed a copy and added it to my take home pile.

How much of a danger were Max and Dean? What were they aiming to achieve? How were the owners of the The Magic Shop involved? My spider senses led me to consider my options. I sent Lara a text, *Have you got time to check out the magic shop first thing tomorrow morning?*

9am?

Perfect

My car wasn't out the back, I remembered Seamus driving over a food laden road to get us here, after an eventful morning. The time hadn't yet struck 5pm, but I wasn't going to be much use to anyone if I couldn't stop yawning. I strolled through the park, attempting to wake myself up. A cluster of elves and fairies waved as I passed them. *Making sure any future magic events are contained...*I heard their words float by me on the wind. I made a mental note to meet with the group at some point. What was the protocol for requesting an audience with elves and fairies?

"Bah!" The man dressed as a green leprechaun stood blocking the path.

"May I pass please?" I asked firmly.

"May I pass please," he mimicked. "No! You can't. What are you going to do about it? Zap me?" He crossed him arms in front of his body, his face scrunched into a frown.

Before I could respond, the group of magical folk moved into a semi-circle in front of me, protecting me from the angry man. They didn't speak. He stared at the group, exasperation on his face. With a blink and a harumph he vanished.

"If you ever need help, just call, and we'll come," The elf I recognised as Brice told me. "We've always been here, but our lore is such that we couldn't approach you, until you displayed your magical strength."

I nodded like I knew what he meant, my mind spinning as my tired brain tried to keep up. I opened my mouth to ask a question, but no words came out.

"It will all make sense, just give it time." The elf added, before the group dispersed. The fairies flew off through the park, the elves, scurried along the paths. I realised I had no idea where elves and fairies called home.

I'm going home, I texted Seamus. I didn't mind walking.

Spark? Can Lexi drive you? I would but somethings come up.

Good plan, I answered, *see you at home later.*

Chapter Twenty-Six

Lexi pulled up behind my car. Nothing appeared disturbed, no packages waiting for me on my verandah. "Thanks Lexi, are you sure you can't come in for a cuppa?"

"Thanks, but I promised Mum I'd help after work setting up for her sister's birthday. Thanks to our detour to the supermarket, I have everything she needed. I'll see you tomorrow." Her back seat piled high with grocery bags, I grabbed the bag of food I'd collected, deciding I needed a sugar fix. I'd never used my magic that way before, and I was still a little worn after the enchantment in the park earlier.

Spark jumped through the front door, sniffing around the door to Grandma's bedroom. "Good job little fella," I shut the front door, dropped my bags on the ground in the hallway, remembering I wanted to check to see if the ledgers and journal had reappeared. I opened the door to Grandma's wardrobe. The empty shelves yelled at me, the knot in my stomach grew bigger as I stared at the emptiness. I closed my eyes, "If Agnes is right, the ledgers are still here," I stepped gingerly towards the wooden shelves with my hands out. I expected my fingers to stretch to the wooden panel at the back of the wardrobe. Instead, my fingers curled around the leather binding of a book, and another, and another, until I'd accounted for all the missing ledgers.

My heart pounded with excitement. Maybe I'd not botched the enchantment after all. Had Dean tried to break in, and the house expelled him back through the window before he could find anything?

I closed the wardrobe door and headed for the bed, turning back to fetch a spare crocheted coat hanger. I draped the colourful patchwork robe over the coat hanger, and tucked the garment into the wardrobe, ensuring the doors were tightly closed. The shiny ornate silver doorknobs caught my eyes, though I'd seen them hundreds of times before. The metal, shaped like a many petaled flower, with weird faces carved in the middle. I swear one of the faces winked at me. "Tiredness," I muttered to myself. The last time I'd seen the journal it sat in the box on Grandma's bed. I closed my eyes, with my hands outstretched. My energy tingled upon feeling the warm red leather between my fingers. "Do I read it now?" I asked my familiar. He patted my ankle with his paw, a sign to follow him. I reluctantly let go of the journal as he led me to the kitchen.

With the kettle boiling, and food in Spark's bowl, I changed out of my black pants and jade shirt, into a pink flannel pyjama set I'd not worn for years. The multi-coloured unicorns and cute kittens made me smile, as I remembered rarely wearing the pyjamas as a sullen teen. I preferred an oversized black t-shirt, or a daggy tracksuit as nighttime clothes. I carried the bags I'd dumped in the hall, into the kitchen. Once the cold meats, cheeses, fruit and biscuits were put away, the chocolate bar and packets of cakes on the bench, I took two carrots out to Buddy. Spark joined me as I sat on the step, letting Buddy nibbles pieces of carrot from my hand. "I could easily curl up in a ball and sleep for hours," I told my furry friends. Promising to visit early in the morning I locked the back door and poured water over a peppermint tea bag. I poured a tall glass of water, draining it before sitting at the table. It took a few seconds for me to realise Jacob had visited, his distinct handwriting stood out on the back of one of the manilla folders on the table.

You are more powerful than I realised. Dean is worried. Be ready — when he works out his next move you will have to act quickly.

Apart from the revelation he thought I was powerful, none of his words came as I surprise. "I know Dean, Max, and your coven are trying to hurt me. Do the owners of the magic shop in town have something to do with the coven? Are Dean and Max planning to build a Majestic Mirage on the Wynyard Street site?" Getting into the habit of talking to my ghostly cousin proved easier than I expected.

Yes, and yes

"Can you give me any more details? Should I be scared of the coven?"

No, I can't – you are protected...but I'm not.

Intuition told me that was all I'd get for tonight at least. "I'm still not sure why Jacob and Dean are in the same coven, or why they are interested in our town," I told my kitten as he chased my toes. "It's curious that he tried to help me to a point. I wonder if it's some ancient family tie that he can't disengage from. The history is a little scarce, though maybe when I read Grandmas journal, I'll figure it out." I munched the gooey chocolate bar, savouring the runny peppermint confectionery hidden inside.

I jumped as the front door opened, though I expected Seamus at any minute. "Hi honey, I'm home," he joked, as he popped a paper bag on the table. "Dessert," he explained with a smile.

"Hang on," I reached into the fridge, and extracted my shopping. Grabbing the handmade wooden cheese board, I roughly chopped the assorted meat and cheeses, adding grapes, berries and dried apricots. Placing it in the middle of the table, I emptied the packet of biscuits into a bowl, adding some cashew nuts and pretzels. "All in date, I promise," knowing Seamus's views on my cooking expertise, and the average age of the items in my kitchen cupboard.

"I appreciate you putting it all together," Seamus voice was scratchy, and he yawned in the middle of his sentence. "It's been such a long day, even my appetite is suffering," he quipped.

"Have a big drink of water," I suggested, bringing two tall glasses of tap water to the table. "It mightn't fix your appetite, but it'll help with dehydration." I picked at the berries I'd placed on my plate, not particularly hungry ether. There was so much I wanted to say, I just didn't have the energy.

"It'll wait 'til the morning," Seamus agreed, quietly, munching on a cheese, cracker and meat sandwich. Spark curled up at my feet as we picked at our cheese board selection. "I think even the muffins will have to wait until the morning. I dropped into the café, and Evie handed me the bag, she'd kept them to one side, as she'd promised." Seamus admitted a few minutes later. "Do you mind if I sleep here, I don't think I should be behind the wheel, even for the short drive home."

My heart beat faster, at the thought of sharing my bed with Seamus for a second night in a row. My skin tingled, I tried to distract myself, clearing the leftovers off the table, returning the food to the fridge for another meal. "You're welcome to stay here anytime," I knew my cheeks were red, and I took solace in the fact he felt the same way, at least he used to. I piled the empty plates and glasses into the sink and ran the hot water. "I'll just wash this up, then I think it's bedtime. If you want to grab a pair of Dad's pyjamas, they'll be some in the long drawers in my parents room. I'll meet you in my room in five minutes."

I felt, rather than heard Seamus behind me, "I promise, it's not too weird," I turned, and saw the look on my friend's face, "Well it is weird, but Dad wouldn't mind," I pulled the plug out of the sink, and walked with him into my parents' room. He stood near the door as Spark, and I walked over to my parent's dresser and opened the bottom drawer. I held up an unopened packet containing blue flannelette pyjamas, swallowing the lump in my throat. "Here you go," I handed the packet to him. Spark and I crossed the hall to my bedroom. I turned on my bedside light on.

"Nice unicorns," Seamus chuckled, diffusing the tension as I hopped into bed. I held out my hand for his, falling asleep a few minutes after my head hit the pillow.

Chapter Twenty-Seven

I couldn't move my arm. My heart thumped as I squeezed opened one eye. As I focused, I realised my arm was tucked under Seamus, sound asleep on the pillow next to me. Spark nuzzled in between us.

In my hazy recollection of my dream, I'd been running from Dean and Max, and Seamus had saved the day. I smiled fondly at my dearest friend, not remembering exactly how he'd pulled it off, but knowing he did. I couldn't imagine life without the man sleeping quietly by my side. I valued our friendship more than any other, and as much as I didn't want to admit to myself, I yearned for our relationship to become more than friends. All the people I loved died, or lied to me, except Seamus. I knew that was a little dramatic, parents, family members, did die, and lie occasionally to protect loved ones. I yawned quietly, so as not to wake him. Spark stretched, his little paw touched my cheek, broadening my smile. He snuggled back down, his back tucked into Seamus's chest. I'd no feeling in my arm, but didn't want to move, lest I ruin the moment. I closed my eyes, deciding to enjoy the peace and quiet.

Just as I began to doze, Seamus's mobile beeped. Mine followed a couple of seconds later. I managed to reach mine with my free arm. *Did you authorise contractors to clean up the Wynyard Street site?* asked Jon.

No, but I should...

Someone already is – Jon replied.

We'll be there asap

"Morning," Seamus whispered, his voice husky after a good six-hour sleep.

"Good morning," I responded, hurriedly pulling on black jeans and a dress shirt, not sure how long we'd be at the site or whether we'd have a chance to change before work. "Jon messaged; someone has authorised contractors on the Wynyard Street site. I forgot to organise anything, and I assume you'd have told me if you had. I'm going there now, to get to the bottom of it. If you want to join me, we can breakfast at the café afterwards." I pulled on black boots over ankle socks. The boots were short, my jean legs sat just low enough not to get caught when I walked.

Seamus leapt to his feet. "Do you think your dad would be okay with me borrowing one of his shirts?" he asked, pulling his jeans on, narrowly missing Spark who bounded off the bed at the same time.

"He would say go right ahead, choose whichever item of clothing you needed," I picked up my phone, and a black cardigan, knowing I'd need it outside in the cool morning air. "I'll make us travel cuppas and feed the four-legged friends." I detoured to the bathroom for a quick freshen up, fed the pets, and was pouring hot water into the plastic travel mugs when Seamus appeared, wearing a bluey mauve shirt.

"It is too much?" he asked, twirling around for me to check the back. Dad's shirts were long sleeved, with cuffs, not the style my farmer friend would normally wear.

"You look very handsome," my cheeks reddened, but I didn't care. I bent to pat my kitten on the head, "You can stay here today, little guy." I handed Seamus the dark blue mug, choosing the bright pink one for myself. "I've my laptop, phone, keys, wallet..."

"What about those?" Seamus pointed to the pile pf papers and the manilla folder.

"Thanks," I scooped them up, shoving them in the side of my bag, grateful I'd chosen the bag a size bigger than my computer, one with a flat bottom, half briefcase, half handbag. "Do we both take our cars?"

"Nah, I can run you back here if you need to go anywhere later," Seamus opened the front door, locking it after me. "I messaged Frank, the contractor. He couldn't talk over the phone, but he'll talk to us on site. Jon's stopped the work from progressing until we get there."

"Thank you." It was handy having a bestie who virtually knew everyone in town.

The next few minutes, we sipped our brews, getting our heads straight for the conversation and day ahead. How did Dean and Max convinced the contractor they owned the site. What sort of identification do you need before employing contractors? Jon's white police car, and a couple of large work utes were parked outside what used to be the little row of five shops, now reduced to charred remains, and indistinguishable rubble.

"Morning Jon, thanks for calling," I approached Jon, as Seamus headed straight to the man with the yellow hard hat, and a bright orange high visibility vest on over an orange shirt and beige overalls I assumed to be Frank.

"Someone called it in, the dozer started before 5am. I headed here straight away, thankfully the, er, other strange events haven't started again, since your, whatever that was at the park yesterday," he replied as Seamus and Frank joined us.

The contractor shook my hand. "Apologies for the misunderstanding. The man on the phone said he was acting on your behalf. Needed the site cleared today, as construction would begin tomorrow. I thought it was odd, but the money was good, and I figured you'd be doing the right thing, not just as mayor, but because of who your family is," the tall man faltered, "I'm not in any trouble, am I?"

It made sense, I guess, contractors wouldn't normally ask for evidence of ownership, necessarily, would they? "You're not in trouble, and I do need the site cleared as it happens. I'll pay you, your normal hourly rate. Do you happen to remember the name of the person who rang you, or even which contractor was starting construction?" I handed Frank one of my business cards, "Just email me the invoice and I'll pay it by the end of the day."

A wave of relief washed over Frank's countenance. He removed his hard hat, wiping his brow with the back of his hand. "Thank you, Beth, I appreciate that. I know the builders are part of that Majestic Mirage group, I had to contact them to check a few specifications – how much ground to scrape, or whether they preferred to concrete pour over the existing base." He fished a crumpled piece of paper out of his pocket. I noticed smudges as he tried to flatten it out, to read it. "I think the man's name was Dan, or maybe Don," he squinted, trying to read his own scrawl.

"Could it have been Dean?" I tried hard to keep my anger in check, it wasn't Frank's fault.

"That was it!" Frank shook his head, "I'm sorry I didn't ask him any more questions, or check with you directly. I'd normally meet face to face, but I figured you'd be busy, and I knew you owned the site." He sighed. Taking a deep breath, he placed the hard hat on his head. "You want the site made safe; do you have any plans for rebuilding?"

"Not at this stage," the knot in my stomach tightened its grip at the idea of rebuilding. "Can you please make it safe, so people can walk around the area safely. Maybe leave one of those temporary fences around the perimeter if it's needed. I can pay the cost of renting the fence for as long as we need." I looked at Seamus, wondering if I'd missed anything.

"Do you have something sturdier than the temp fences? Noting the interest in the area, I'd like to have a system we can lock, making it harder for intruders." I knew my friend would know the right thing to do, I smiled at him appreciatively.

Frank pulled an old dusty mobile phone out of the pocket of his overalls. "Nah, sorry, we only use the temp ones, I could ring around some places if you like."

"It's okay, I know who to call," Seamus scrolled through his phone's contact list, "Ah, here it is," he pressed a button, walking to one side to speak to the person who answered.

I turned to Frank, "Any problem, please ring me straight away, my numbers on my business card." I did my best to ignore the lump in my throat, and the knot in my stomach that tightened every time I caught a glimpse of the destruction caused by the arsonist. My mind tried to make sense of the twisted burnt items my eyes saw, equating the items with what I remembered of my visits to each store.

As Frank returned to work, I caught Jon before he hopped into his car. "Have I missed anything? Do I need to fill out any paperwork, fill in any forms? I'm trying to work out what else I neglected."

"I don't think so. Now that Spirit Town isn't being inundated with magical mischiefs, we'll investigate Max and Dean, to see if there's anything from a legal standpoint." He scribbled a note on his notepad. "I'm assuming they know how to stay just within the law or at least have a lawyer who can talk their way out of anything. Be careful," he added as he opened the door to his police car.

"I will," I promised, hoping I'd be able to stick to that promise, as the day progressed.

Chapter Twenty-Eight

A flash blue pickup truck pulled up as I headed over to Seamus. "Do you remember Marc?" he asked, "In our year at school." I nodded my hello, vaguely remembering Marc as one of Seamus's basketball pals. "He can help us with security fencing. He designed and trialled a high security fencing on his property. He's growing ginger, turmeric, garlic, in greenhouses and he was worried about vandalism. Mainly curiosity visitors, it's the first farm in the area to grow these types of crops. Since setting up the fencing there's been no more problems."

"Is it just where the shops stood, or the carpark out back?" Mark asked, piling himself out of his vehicle. He stood over six foot tall, the perfect height for a basketballer. Tuffs of ginger hair hung on either side of the cap he wore backwards. His headgear unashamedly advertising *Ginger Farms*.

"The car park, and the old park area on the other side, all belongs to my...to me." My words caught in my throat.

"No wonder you want to secure it, its prime land for redevelopment." Marc nodded as he snapped some pictures with his mobile. Was he trustworthy? How well did Seamus really know him? My arm tingled as Seamus touched my arm for long enough to catch my eye and nod. Okay, if Seamus trusted him, I guess I did too.

"Ball park figure for securing it, with a lock system only Seamus and I will need to use?" I crossed my fingers, hoping for a reasonable cost I could manage.

"If it's for Seamus, I won't charge you at all." My eyes widened; not quite sure I heard correctly. "I've been trying to pay him back for years. He did he a huge favour once and he won't accept anything in return. Reckons he doesn't need my system on the farm, and he's probably right." He grinned like he was ten years old and won a game of marbles.

I glanced from Marc to Seamus, his hands on his hips pretending to be mad at Marc. "Okay, thanks, I'm not sure how I can pay you back for your generosity. Do you want to join us for breakfast at Evie's Café?"

"Thanks, but I've got a busy day ahead. Maybe another time. When you do need this secure, as soon as Frank finishes, I guess?"

"If you can, that'd be perfect," I agreed.

Marc's mobile rang as he climbed into the cab of his work truck. I watched him drive off, talking into his phone, wondering what favour Seamus had bestowed that Marc was so eager to repay.

Seamus tapped me on the arm. "Um, breakfast, I'm still up for that," he held up the blue travel mug, "This was great and all, but..."

I pulled my eyes away from the scene in front of me. All that remained of the shops my parents were so proud of. I still felt the warmth of the camaraderie between Dad and the men's shed guys. The eager, excited conversations between mum, and the other women over coffee in the laundrette. The echo of the past lingered, even in the unidentifiable rubble. Determined not to give in to the melancholy, I forced my mouth into a smile. "Breakfast yes! Let's go."

The doorbell jangled as Seamus and I entered the café. The clock told me school hadn't yet started, accounting for the number of youth lined up in front of us. "It feels later than just after eight," I whispered.

"That's because Jon messaged us at 6am," Seamus stifled a yawn. "I was having such a nice dream," he murmured. The heat rose in my cheeks, a sensation I was becoming familiar with these days. The colour drained from my face a few seconds later, when I spied Max and Dean perched at the Wi-Fi bench, munching bacon and egg burgers. Two large takeaway mugs sat beside their plates. Seamus gave my hand a quick squeeze. I allowed the connection to calm my energy. Toying with the idea of confronting them, instead I turned to Seamus and mouthed thank you.

The eight or so youths who'd each ordered chocolate chip muffins and milk shakes, nodded to Dean as they left. My nemesis caught me staring and looked away, pretending to be interested in what Max was saying. A couple of women joined the line behind us. I recognised Lily Hindmarsh, the town's librarian. "Hi Beth, Seamus, it's lovely to see you. I've been suggesting to everyone who comes into the library, that they attend Friday's meeting. I hope the town gets behind Jan and the others. I've a couple of ideas I'd like to run past you both." Lily's long navy dress sat just above the ground. I noticed she was wearing the shiny black boots I admired last time I saw her wearing them.

"Why don't you send me an email with a time that suits you, and we can come by the library," I enjoyed meeting Lily when I'd first returned to town, she had lots of ideas and positive energy, I wasn't sure what her powers were, but elves helped in the library, so chances were she possessed special skills.

As we approached the counter, Max's raised voice permeated the space. "When I was mayor, I never went to work in jeans, not even fancy black jeans," He sneered loudly his hand waving in my general direction to emphasize his point.

A half snort escaped my mouth. So tempted to mention pot bellies and crumpled shirts with askew ties, but I didn't. Bessie swung through the door to the kitchen, overhearing our ex-mayors comment she said in a loud aside to her daughter, "Don't you just love Beth's look. It's casual, approachable, always clean, tidy, ironed, she never looks like she's just climbed out of bed and tumbled to work." She gave me a wink, as she backed through to the kitchen.

Seamus ran his finger along the breakfast menu propped up in a plastic frame on the counter. I heard the barely contained chuckle in his voice, "Love your Mum Evie. Can we please have a chicken and bacon wrap each, with a side serve of berries, and two mochas."

Evie smiled. Today her hair was tied in circular plaits on either side of her head above her ears. She wore a bright pink pinafore with a black top underneath. The black shirt sleeves rolled up. "Coming right up. Why don't you sit near the kitchen? The fairies are just cleaning the table now."

"Sounds good," Seamus handed over the money before I'd fished my wallet out of my bag. I watched a couple of fairies, dressed in a shimmery silver material that rendered the creatures nearly invisible, as they wove a line of fairy dust near Max and Dean. The men were too busy trying to outdo each other, talking loudly about fishing and golf, to notice. The other café patrons were surreptitiously watching the magical creatures, so as not to alert the two men.

I slid into the red leather seat and smiled. Sprinkled in fairy dust on the table were the words *cone of silence*. Seamus chuckled as he read the words created from hundreds of tiny colourful specks. Lily swung past our table on the way out and handed us each a mug from her carry box. "Bessie will bring your food over soon," she beamed as she read the fairy scrawl. "I'll email you as soon as I can, it'll be after 10am, I think I'm free between 11am and 2pm but I'll confirm that."

"What is it?" Seamus asked, following my gaze. "Ah..." he acknowledged. The man in green, from the magic shop, still dressed in green, had joined Max and Dean. As another man dressed in a black suit joined them, they moved to a table at the opposite end to the café to where we were sitting.

"Don't worry, the fairies have a way of recording pertinent bits of information," Bessie told us, placing plates in front of us. "We don't advertise that, for obvious reasons. Mostly what they pick up on just floats away on the breeze in a million bits and pieces, unless it's important. Enjoy, and if you need anything, just ask."

Chapter Twenty-Nine

We decided to divide and conquer. Seamus headed to his saddlery to answer a question posed by a customer. My plan to head to the office and check my email interrupted when Lara texted, that she was on her way to *The Magic Shop*. I met her outside the shop, "Thanks for reminding me, it's been a bit of a whirlwind. I'd like to say that life isn't always like this around here, but I'm beginning to wonder."

Lara took my arm as I went to open the door, "Before we go in, let's walk up the street for a while," she led me away from shop, "I've been visiting Agnes. She's doing okay," she added, as I opened my mouth to ask. "She shared some information with me, personal information I need to share with you, not now, it'd take hours, maybe we could meet later." Lara paused; I felt her nerves through her shaking hands. "Agnes did say that she thought the owners of the magic shop were related to one of the families in Spirit Town. Like you and Jacob are related. Elemental magic, that's what she said."

I stopped, turning Lara to face me, "Are you okay? You're shaking. Is there something else? We're friends, you can tell me anything." My friend turned pale, then red, I thought she may faint, so I led her to one of the old-fashioned wooden benches dotted along the footpath.

She sat, pulled me down next to her. "It's Agnes, she's my aunt. Her sister, Madeline was my mother. The rest of the story, it's too much for now, but I wanted you to know that." She took a long breath, pulling her back straight, squaring her shoulders. "Okay, let's go meet some magicians."

Her smile slipped a little. I tucked my arm in hers. "We're off to see the wizard," I grinned, making her giggle.

The doorbell chimed in a deep tone I didn't remember from my only other visit a few weeks ago. The walls, and floors were painted black, the ceiling painted ruby red, with velvet curtains both red and black, hanging in various positions throughout the space. Dark wooden shelves full of every type of child's magic tricks I could think of lined the walls. Cups and balls, cards, wands, top hats, capes, white rabbits, rope, chains, cages, flowers, hankies, dice, could all be bought separately or in sets.

At the front of the counter the man in green stood, a woman in a bright red dress sat on a stool behind the tall, cabinet unit that doubled as a countertop. A crystal ball sat on a red velvet cloth in between them, a deck of cards under the woman's long slender fingers. Her long black nails shone with glitter nail polish.

"Excuse me, my name is Beth, and this is Lara," I didn't get finish my sentence.

"We know who you are," the man grumbled.

"Come now Finn, behave," the woman admonished him, then held out her hand to in our general direction. "I'm Maeve. This is my brother Finn. We used to live in Spirit Town, until our parents moved away to the big city for work. We decided to visit a few months ago and fell in love with the place. Sold up in the city and moved here." She poked her brother in the chest. "Finn here, always wanted to own a shop, and when we saw there was no magic shop in Spirit Town, well it just seemed perfect. He's an accountant, so he's good for numbers. I dabble in all sorts, fortune telling, mind reading, and I teach." I suppressed a smile, thinking Morticia would be a more appropriate name then Maeve. I swallowed quietly, remembering mind reading was one of her skills.

Lara ran her finger over the velvet cloth. "Do either of you have elemental magical ability?" Her voice faltered. "I'm only asking, because

I'm new too, from the city, and I'm still getting used to the place. If you teach, maybe I can sign up for some lessons."

Finn glared at me, before stomping off into the back room, through a black curtain so thick it hardly moved as he pushed himself through it. "Don't mind him," Maeve laughed off his behaviour, "he's been extra grumpy lately. We're from a family blessed, or cursed, with magical gifts." She stared into one of the corners of her shop, as if listening for a distant sound, or maybe she saw movement on the shelf full of top hats.

"Are there more magic kits through the curtain?" I was glad Lara asked, she made the question sound innocent, I would've sounded accusatory, as if I knew they were trying to hide something.

"No." I thought that was all the information Maeve would share, "That's where we run classes, workshops for those interested in practising their craft. A bit of fun is all..." after another long pause she continued, "is there anything else I can help you with?"

I glanced around the shop, walked over to the shelf promoting – *the only magic kit you'll ever need.* "If I bought one of these kits today, can I book into your next class? I'm sure I'll need help figuring it out." I felt Lara's nerves jangle the longer we stood in the space. It felt increasingly cloying, as if it were sucking the air from our bodies.

"Sure, I can put your names on our waiting list, our workshops are very popular." She slid a large black ledger across to me. A pen sat in the nook in the middle of the open page. "Write your name and contact details, and we'll be in touch when there's a free spot." Hundreds of tiny feet crawling up my spine, or so it felt to me, urging me not to write in Maeve's register.

I touched Lara's hand, muttering the words of a protection spell, lest we leave the store with some unwanted energies, or worse. Maeve's eyes bore into mine, leaving me under no illusion that she knew exactly what I was doing. She knew from the determination in mine, that she wasn't going to mess with me or my friend.

Luckily my mobile rang. "I'm sorry, I have to take this," I held up my phone, "I'll be back when I get a chance," Lara and I covered the distance to the door in record time, as I pressed the green button, "Hello, Beth speaking," my voice almost drowned by the ominous bell sound as we escaped into the fresh air and bright sunshine on the other side.

Chapter Thirty

After making sure Lara hadn't suffered any obvious side effects of our time in the store, and promising to catch up after work, I headed straight to my mayoral office. "What's happened?" I asked breathless from the brisk walk.

Seamus looked up from his computer. "What? Oh, nothing much, my intuition told me you needed an escape. Where were you? You seemed...fuzzy..."

I flopped into the halfway decent comfy client chair positioned opposite his posh black leather chair. The type of furniture that would've adorned the mayoral office, if Max hadn't removed it all when he ran away. "I ran into Lara; we ducked into *The Magic Shop*...it was an experience and thank you...you rang at the perfect time and saved us from...something." I shuddered at the memory. "I'll explain more later. Did we hear from Lily?"

"That was the other reason why I rang." Seamus consulted his watch. A silver timepiece I vaguely remembered my parents giving him when we graduated. "We're due to the library in...just under an hour."

"What? How long were we gone? It felt like maybe twenty minutes." Lara and I headed into the magic store just after 9am. I blinked as I noticed the clock on the wall telling me it was close to eleven.

Seamus shook his head, "Try over an hour, maybe more if you went there straight after the café. I couldn't get through to you the first three times I rang, and I had to move a morning meeting to just after lunch.

The others were okay about it, I told them Max was interfering with the clean-up at Wynyard Street, which wasn't an outright lie."

"Oh my...okay well, what else did I miss?" I pushed away the concern that Lara and I had been in the shop for such a long time without realising it.

"I may have just solved one of our problems," Seamus grinned like someone just offered him free food.

"Do tell," I rummaged in my bag, wishing I'd thought to bring a bottle of water.

"In the cupboard behind you," Seamus prompted. I opened the wood panelled door, surprised to find a small fridge, with a few bottles of water. I nodded my thanks. "It's been bothering me that Dean and Max are meeting so openly. They're taunting us, expecting us to confront them. Majestic Mirage the company, has several shareholders. It's not set up like any other company I've seen. I've a mate who left town years ago, works in the city. His research methods are a little unusual. He managed to pull apart the layers of lies and deception. Max Graham is a shareholder, so is Dean Collier, and Finn O'Riley,"

"From the magic shop," I interjected.

"Yes, there's more. Your cousin is a stakeholder too."

"Jacob?"

"Afraid so,"

"He's part of Dean's coven, or rather he said they were part of a coven...I don't suppose your friend could figure out the other members?"

"Exactly what I've been thinking. It's not a coven in the historical sense of the word. Apparently, everyone who is exiled from Spirit Town, is invited to join an exclusive club. Traditionally exiled meant told to leave by your parents, grandmother, and your ancestors who lived before them. Max sought Dean out when you returned to town, pre-empting an altercation," Seamus scratched the back of his head. "This's where it gets trickier to decipher. Jacob misrepresented a few other facts. The coven or club does have overseas members, it's base appears fluid, and it appears there are members living within Spirit Town itself. Not all their members are exiled townsfolk."

"Smoke and mirrors," I commented. "Something about Finn and Mauve, they were acting their roles, like characters in a movie. It wouldn't surprise me if they looked nothing like their current appearance. Didn't Agnes mention it was unclear who owned the shop?"

Seamus typed furiously on his keyboard. I leant over, reading the questions he sent off to his friend in the city, asking him to investigate the names we had for the owners of the magic shop.

A thumping began at my temples, a sign my body and brain were trying to process the huge dump of information. I drained the rest of the water from the plastic bottle. "If the coven, the club, is that insidious, what hope do we have of winning? It appears banishing individuals doesn't work. Would a truce be possible?" I shook my head, blinking to try and make sense of what we were faced with.

My friend stood. "Let's go meet Lily, I get the feeling we need to be on our toes around town, and so the more people who are keen to help us the better. I'm pretty sure most people around town would support us, if they understood what was going on."

"We need to understand it first," I tripped, as I stood, feeling a little lightheaded, I held onto the chair.

"Are you okay?" Seamus eyes me with concern, bridging the gap quickly.

Touching the back of my head, my neck moved stiffly, as if I'd been hit on the head. "I think so, maybe I slept the wrong way," I wished my cheeks didn't redden every time I spoke of sleeping with Seamus. "I don't need food, yet," I jumped in, before Seamus suggested some sustenance might solve the problem.

Thankfully the short walk to the library proved uneventful. "I'm so pleased you made it, please come and sit," She motioned to one of half a dozen tables dotted throughout the space.

The library had benefited from a makeover since I'd lived in Spirit Town, sleek sliding doors replacing the old wooden ones I walked through countless times over the years as a teen and book nerd. The extension, that stretched out towards the rear carpark, was mainly glass panelling. The windows and the cream paint on the walls projected the illusion of space, in a building that was nearing one hundred years old. Shelves lined the walls, strategically placed to allow room for tables and chairs, a comfy reading space, a children's corner and a large front counter.

"Ted will look after the front desk while we chat." A tallish elderly gentleman dressed in navy trousers and a pale blue shirt nodded from his seat behind the counter. His neat white hair and red tie added to the image in my head of retired businessman. "Ted's one of our volunteers. My library assistant, Jade, is finishing some tasks in the storeroom. She's not far away if Ted needs help."

"Thank you for taking the time to meet with us," I smiled. Lily was easy to like, she had a way about her, that made me wonder what her powers were. Not just because her clothing harked back of medieval times with her long flowing dresses, high black boots, her long black ringlets, her personality...it was like I'd found a kindred spirit.

"I'm pleased you could make time to chat with me. I won't take up too much of your time, and I'll send you an email to cover the key points, so you don't have to take notes," she added as I pulled my notepad and pen out of the pocket of my cardigan.

A young mother holding the hands of two small children walked past, towards the children's books section. Lily waved at the little ones. A little elf in blue overalls intercepted the family and bowed. The children giggled and followed the elf, who led them to a shelf of books. "We are fortunate to live in such a friendly town. It's such a shame about what happened in Wynyard Street, I've been thinking about how we could help the tenants." She handed Seamus and I hand drawn maps of what was now a vacant block in Wynyard Street. "I have dreams, or maybe visions is a better word. The revamp of the library was based on one. Anyway, I've tried drawing what I saw," she pointed out some key images on the page. "The middle of the block is a little green space with a small playground, a plaque on the garden setting, with your family name on it," she paused, "I was thinking a handmade wooden setting, like those your dad used to make."

My fingers tingled with an emotion I couldn't quite name. "I love that idea!" I clasped my hands together. Beside me, Seamus nodded his agreement. "What are the squares, here, here and here?" My finger ran around the outside of the map.

"I looked up prices for small portable buildings. There are some nice small buildings available for under ten thousand dollars. I thought the seamstress, laundrette and wood shop would suit those style buildings, and if we were creative, there are sheds or containers that could be converted to shops for the other two." She picked up an A4 folder that sat on the table. "I've all the prices, and ideas for who could help us build it," she placed the folder back on the table. "Just my idea, of course. It's not up to me, but I thought this might work as a starting point for the meeting on Friday." Lily sat back in her chair, A couple of elves in blue walked past our table towards the front of the library, as an elderly couple entered. Seamlessly, the elves slid a couple of chairs on wheels over to the couple, who sat down easily, as if they performed the same action many times before. Each elf stood behind a chair and pushed the couple over to the general fiction section. "I've still no idea why the elves have chosen to help me and the residents when they visit the library, but I'm so grateful they do."

Chapter Thirty-One

"Lily's idea is terrific," Lara agreed. I gave her a brief rundown of the discussion at the library while Seamus ordered lunch. Jon arrived at the table as Seamus returned.

"Lucky you're here mate; I ordered four sets of lunch and cuppas." Seamus joked. "Seriously, has your day been any easier, without all the magic goings on?" He slid in the seat next to me, as Jon sat next to Lara.

"Quiet, but I'm still worried about Max and Dean," Jon fiddled with his notepad, "Every time I think I'm getting somewhere, the trail leads nowhere."

Seamus sat back against the leather back of the booth. "I might be able to help you with that, I've had some luck with figuring it out."

Lara raised her hand, "Before you tell us, may I say something?" she wiggled in her seat, like an excited child who'd just been told some happy news. Knowing what she may be wanting to tell the table; I nodded she should continue. The other two did the same. "I've spent some time with Agnes, since she returned from hospital, she home is amazing by the way...anyway, she, Agnes, told me she knew my mother...that she, Agnes, is my aunt." She flopped back in her seat.

I hopped out of my seat and squeezed Lara into a half hug, nearly toppling us over. "I'm so happy for you, you've found your family. I know it's a lot to take in, I'm here if you ever want to talk." I released Lara from my embrace, and landed back on my seat, just as Bessie arrived with four chicken burgers.

"Thanks Bessie," Seamus high fived our waitress, Bessie beamed at him, blushing like a schoolgirl with a crush.

Jon looked at Lara, rather than his food. "I'd like to hear the whole story, when you're ready to talk about it," he briefly touched her arm, smiled, then returned to his plate. "Thanks for lunch. I didn't realise it, but I'm starving."

"Enjoy it, you work harder than all of us, keeping the town safe. A mate of mine, who works in the city, shed light on some things. He identified Dean, Max, amongst others, as involved with the Majestic Mirage corporation and belong to a group of people who bear a grudge against Beth's family." I heard the seething protectiveness as the weight of the implication weighed heavily on him.

I placed my burger back on my plate and poured four glasses of water from the jug on the table, "Gee, when you put it that way, maybe I should be worried." The lump in my stomach returned. I knew I should eat something before the afternoon council meeting. I nibbled at one corner of the burger.

Seamus cocked his head to one side, "I don't think they'll hurt you directly. For reasons unclear as yet, it appears Jacob wouldn't let them. Max, and Dean are more about discrediting you, making you feel like staying home and not helping the residents of Spirit Town."

A pair of fairies, wearing pretty pink dresses flew over to the kids' corner, trailing sparkling streamers behind them. As they reached the table of four girls, also dressed in layers of tulle, the streamers turned into a basket of presents, wrapped in paper of seven different shades of pink. As I watched the innocent smiles on the faces of the children, an idea came to me. "Then we need to weave some magic and discredit them, with kindness." The others leant in as I continued. "What if, instead of telling everyone that Max and Dean were behind the fire, we invited them, and everyone that my ancestors banished, to return and live in Spirit Town?" The other three stared at me, as if I'd suddenly sprouted two heads. I couldn't blame them, even I thought my idea was a little unconventional. I paused, drinking the refreshing water, letting it cool my burning throat.

Seamus placed his burger back on his plate, "You know how to ruin someone's appetite. You don't mean to ask them all to live at your place, do you?"

I swiped at his shoulder, missing it on purpose. "I only invite very close friends to stay at my place." That my cheeks didn't redden, was a blessing, that Seamus blushed underneath the stubble on his cheeks was even better. "I'd bet that most of the people we're talking about, still own residences here. We invite them to return, it's up to them to choose to take us up on the offer."

"I like it, as a way of distracting them, catching them off guard, and showing we're better than them." Lara spoke quietly. "This town is amazing, everyone is welcoming, friendly, and fierce when they have to be."

My mobile beeped, I noticed a missed call from Izzie. The sight of my food made me nauseous, even the smell of the coffee caused my stomach to flip flop. "I've got to get this, it's Izzie," I nodded at Seamus. "I know, we're meeting at council in twenty minutes, I'll head straight there. Thanks everyone, maybe we can meet at mine later tonight. I'm not offering to cook, just a chance to finish the conversation." I left the others to finish their lunch and dialled Izzie's number.

"Beth! Are you okay? Dean and Max are annoying Lexi, not that she'd ever admit it, but she's shaken by their emails." My friend sounded busy. She woke before 4am each morning and rarely went to bed before midnight. Her following at the radio station was a testament to her hard work.

"Thank for telling me! I'll talk to her straight away. I'll tell her to go home and ignore all the work stuff for the rest of the day. Also, are you free about 6pm tonight? If so, can you call up to my place, I'll ask Lexi to join us." Izzie promised she'd try to make it. As I went to dial Lexi's number, I realised I'd walked to the newspaper office.

I opened the door, and enveloped Lexi in a hug. "I'm so sorry they're being pains in the neck. Have you tried blocking their emails? I have a meeting this afternoon or I'd work from here." I looked around the office, anxious at the thought of her here by herself, with Dean and Max sending threatening emails to her via the newspapers email address. "It's only Wednesday, please take the afternoon off, take your granny to a movie or something. If you're free around six though, pop up to mine, Izzie will be there too. I have some ideas I need to run past you and it's the earliest I can make it." Lexi's eyes filled with tears. "Please don't cry, I'm okay, I don't know what they've been saying, but I'm safe and it will all be sorted soon."

Lexi nodded, extracting a tissue from the box on her desk. "There is a new movie at the cinema I'd been promising to take Granny to." She sniffed into the tissue. "You're the best, Beth," she sniffled.

"Now, come on, I'm supposed to be at my other office, it's twice today I've gone awol, Seamus will have a conniption if I'm late again."

Lexi giggled. "Go on, I'm right behind you, I just have to check the back door's locked."

"Okay, send me a text when you get home, please. I may be over-reacting but I think of you as family." I jangled the bell as I exited the door, jogging to the council office. I was out of practice, I used to walk everywhere, before I became mayor and had no time for anything.

Chapter Thirty-Two

A little out of breath, I picked up my laptop and a bottle of water from my office, on the way to the conference room. I inhaled, held my breath and exhaled a couple of times in an attempt to appear in control as I entered the room. Seamus frowned at me; relief written on his face as I took my seat opposite him. Jamie and Glen were already seated. Kim and Greg arrived a few seconds later.

"Thank you all for agreeing to change the meeting time, so I could be here. This morning was unavoidable. Max and Dean had engaged contractors to work on the Wynyard Street site. They seem to be doing all they can to discredit me," I opened my laptop. "I know that's not why we're here. Is there an update to the local developments?"

Jamie picked up a pile of papers in front of him, handing a bundle of papers to each of us seated around the table. "The agricultural college, it appears Dean Collier would like to help with the funding. Noting that he is in one of the corporations affiliated with Majestic Mirage, we don't want his money. I propose we deny his offer, nicely."

Seamus glanced at me, for my approval, of what he wanted to say. I moved my fingers, in front of me, a code we used years ago, at high school. Two fingers meant go for it. "Instead of refusing their offer, why don't we accept it?" The others around the table frowned at Seamus, as if he'd gone mad. "Hear me out, we're not funding the project ourselves. The local farmers are the strength behind the proposal, and it's them who'll be doing all the hard work. Yes, they're receiving a couple of government grants, and we are working on the roads and infrastructure, but I'm sure they're up for community involvement. We should at least give them the option to consider his proposal. I can talk to Marc and the other farmers and report back tomorrow morning." He glanced at me, and I nodded my confirmation. "Leave it up to the community to decide. Our legal team could ensure any donations don't allow the gifter any voting power or shares in the college, or anywhere else." The four seated around the table conferred, murmuring amongst themselves. Greg stared over his glasses at Seamus a couple of times.

Jamie turned to me, "Do you support this idea, in light of everything that's happened to you?"

"That's a fair question. The thought of Max or Dean having any involvement in Spirit Town gives me the heebie jeebies, but they aren't going away. They've supporters in town. You know my parents, and grandmother before that, exiled people for using their magic in a way that was detrimental to the town?" The others nodded that yes, they knew about that part of the Spirit Town story. "Well, it appears that Dean and Max have befriended those people. If we freeze them out totally, as I'd love to do, they'll just keep coming at us. Why not offer them a place in town, invite them to return and be a part of the community? I want to talk to Agnes before formalising this proposal, and I'm interested in your thoughts. Is it something you see we could support?"

"Speaking only for myself, I'd have to think about it. We'd have to make the terms clear, to live abiding the laws, using magic the right way, that sort of thing," Glen mused. "What if we meet next Monday afternoon to discuss further?"

I typed a few strokes on my keyboard, setting myself a reminder to call into see Agnes as soon as possible and to make a formal written proposal available to the others by the end of the week. "Sounds good thanks. What else is on the agenda?" The remainder of the meeting passed uneventfully. Each council member gave an update of how their area of expertise was progressing. I made notes and tried my best to pay attention to what they were saying. My mind kept wandering, as my eyes moved around the room, my intuition checking for any hidden bugs. There were a few spots around the table and the cupboards that ran the length of the room. I stood, running my hands around the edges of the furniture, feeling for tiny metal discs.

"I think she's searching for listening devices." Seamus offered, as my behaviour caused raised eyebrows.

"The good news is, I don't think the room is bugged." I leant to look under the edge of the side cabinet. "I found bugs in my office a couple of days ago, and meant to check in here, but forgot." I admitted.

"Luckily I remembered," Seamus pulled out a bottle of water with three little metal blobs floating in it. "I just forgot to tell you."

After the meeting adjourned, Seamus trailed me to my office. "They were more open to the idea than I thought."

"At least they didn't laugh us out of the room and have white coated men cart us away in straight jackets." I agreed. "This morning seems such a long time ago, remind me, did we take two cars, or one?"

Seamus gave me that look – the *I don't know what I'm going to do with you* – look. "I drove. I suppose you'd like me to drop you at Agnes's to tell her our thoughts, before the grapevine does."

"You're the best, Seamus, have I ever told you that?" I clapped my hands together in glee.

"Not nearly often enough," he grumbled, with a smile on his face.

"Oh, and we've got Lara, Jon, Izzie and Lexi coming over around 6pm," I added with my best butter wouldn't melt in my mouth expression.

"We have, have we?" Seamus stuck his hands on his hips then waggled his finger at me, "So am I helping you convince Agnes that letting a whole lot of exiled residents to live within the town limits is a good idea, or am I heading to the supermarket for food to feed the hordes?"

I crinkled my eyes, trying to look innocent, and whispered "Both?" adding in a normal voice "I know you could manage both, and your ability to find, create, make edible food far surpasses any attempts I've ever made."

"You're right there, grab your stuff and let's get going then. We've got just over an hour."

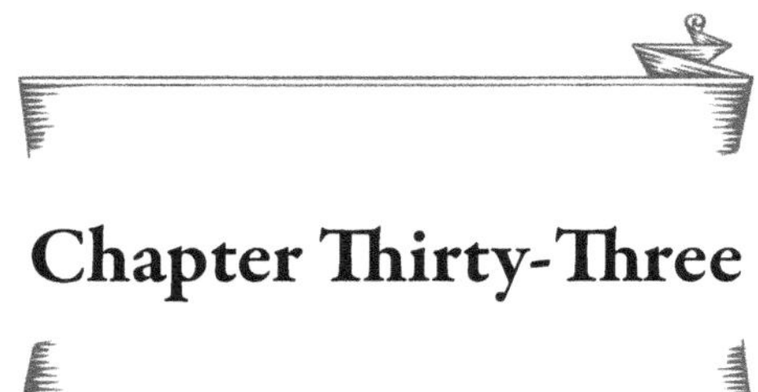

Chapter Thirty-Three

As we pulled Seamus's vehicle into a space outside Agnes's house, I saw her, sitting in her rocking chair, on her verandah, with a thick woollen blanket over her legs, a beanie on her head, and a scarf wrapped around her neck. All three garments were likely knitted by her, the wool was a fluffy mohair greeny-brown that looked cozy. I felt tears forming in the corners of my eyes. She generally looked younger than her seventy years, today, sitting all rugged up, she appeared frail, vulnerable. I revised that thought as we moved closer, and I noticed the scowl on her face.

"The two of you are bright, I taught you both, and I know you haven't lost your marbles, so come, tell me what's going on." She motioned we should sit on the chairs positioned to face her. It felt like we were back at high school, in trouble, we both quickly sat down.

"Who told you?" I asked, wondering at my voice, sounding like I was about five years old and caught in the act of sneaking a biscuit off the cooling rack.

"Who told me? Why the moment you both thought about it, ripples started. Whispers carried on the wind. I don't need to hear it from anyone's lips, except yours." Her scowl still caused my toes to curl in my boots.

"It seemed logical, once we figured out how big the coven / club is, and that Dean and Max are part of the group of people exiled from town. They'll continue to make life difficult for everyone in Spirit Town, simply because they can. If, instead of trying to send them away, we invite them and the others who've been exiled, to return, if they want to, we are taking away their power. We invite them to be a part of the community, and apply strict but fair rules and boundaries. We're hoping they'll either come back and live happily or leave and cause trouble somewhere else. Please tell us we're not totally deluded." My legs were doing that wibbly wobbly wiggle they did all my themselves, when I was nervous. I didn't dare take my eyes off Agnes to see how Seamus fared.

"Hmm...Beryl was right all those years ago, when we were watching you both in the playground during a school celebration. She insisted you'd both achieve great things. I thought she was being soft, grand-motherly, goo-ing and gaa-ing over the two of you. You were only about six at the time." My eyes bugged when I realised, she'd just thrown us a compliment and that in part she agreed with our thoughts. I allowed myself a sideways glance at Seamus. His wide eyes assured me he was just as surprised as I. "There's just one thing," she continued a little less huffily, but still with that schoolteacher's voice that terrified so many of our peers, "You will need to show the strength of your magic. Mainly you Beth, but Seamus, don't be surprised if you are called on too. How you choose to do so is up to you, but it needs to be public."

My brain didn't know what to do with that piece of information, other than acknowledging Agnes was right of course. Seamus recovered quicker than I. "Changing the subject Agnes, how are you feeling? We may have come to tell you our thoughts and ask for your opinion, but over and above that we do both care about you." His voice, also a little wobbly, told me maybe he'd not recovered after all.

"I know that young Quinn, or you'd be clipped around the ears and sent on your way. I'm fine. Tomorrow I'll be moving around as if noth-ing ever happened. First thing in the morning I'll talk to Mike and the others, and let you know of any concerns, so you have time before the meeting the next day. Now you'd better hop to it, or you won't be home to feed your visitors."

It was uncanny how she *just knew* stuff. It didn't freak me out now, as much as when I was a teenager, although I suspected Seamus still got spooked. "Thank you, Agnes. We're glad you're on the mend, and I'm sure we'll talk tomorrow sometime." I wanted to hug her but settled for squeezing her hands as they lay on her lap. She smiled, knowing our hearts, our emotions, without us whispering a word.

"A magical show of strength," Seamus muttered as he backed out onto the road, shaking his head in disbelief. "Easier question, what's for dinner, for six people?"

I thought about the layout of the supermarket, how busy it'd be, and the time that remained. "What about a couple of hot chickens, some salad, bread rolls, and a couple of packets of lamingtons for dessert?"

"I see what you're thinking, good plan," Seamus said admiringly. "If you grab all that I can grab a couple of other goodies and meet you at the self-serve."

I snorted, "Yeah right, only if you don't stop to talk to everyone along the way."

He looked mortally wounded, "I promise, I pinkie-promise swear," he held out his left hand, extending the pinkie. I laughed, as he pulled the ute into a spare spot right in front of the supermarket.

"Okay go!" I pointed to my watch as we entered the bustling supermarket.

"It was hilarious," I told the group gathered around the kitchen table, half an hour later. "Watching him trying to be polite and not offend everyone but get back to the self-serve in time to get back here before 6pm."

Seamus gave me a look, meant to be a frown, but his twinkling eyes gave his feelings away. I knew mine were doing the same. We probably should have a talk about our feelings, Seamus would honour my earlier instructions, that we were just friends, until the day he died, unless I shared with him that I thought that maybe, we could be something else. A red blush passed over my cheeks. I busied myself with preparing the salad.

Lara, stood beside me, pouring six tall glasses of ginger beer. The drinks were her contribution to this evening's festivities. "Agnes agreed with your proposal?" I'd just told the gathering about the plan Seamus and I concocted, to welcome back those exiled, if they wanted to return. "Are you sure...I mean about your plan...it's bold..."

"As sure as I am about anything." I flopped on the seat between Lexi and Seamus. Spark, purring loudly on Lexi's lap reassuringly tapped my knee with his paw. "We can't keep on with this dance of drama, damage, vandalism etc."

Lara passed the plate of bread rolls to her right. Jon chose one and passed it on to Izzie. "How do we know that it won't be seen as invitation to behave badly, causing more problems for the town?" Jon questioned, as he spread a thin layer of salad on the bottom of his roll.

"Yeah, we don't...we may need some help with the details..." Seamus sighed. "It seemed like a good idea, it still does. Isn't there a rule with naughty children where we are supposed to give them positive attention or give them something meaningful to do...something along those lines..." he left his thought hanging as he loaded some chicken into his bread roll.

I couldn't tell if the butterflies in my stomach were caused by the worry about our proposal, or the incredibly handsome man sitting to my left. I looked into the eyes of my second oldest friend. "What do you think Izzie?"

My reporter friend put down the burger she'd been holding. "Totally bonkers, since the first day I met you. But your idea certainly has merit. I do have a question, what big show of power do you propose? I think it may be the key to whether this whole caper works or not. Before we solve that, can we eat first? Poor Seamus looks like he'll fade away to nothing soon," she winked at me as she resumed eating.

Everyone followed her lead. "Thanks, I think," Seamus mumbled, before devouring his dinner.

I looked around the table at my friends as I ate my burger. All different, I loved each one of them, and not just because they always had my back. They didn't judge me or say I should do or be something I wasn't. Each one encouraged me to believe in myself. "It strikes me that the power of our town is in our ability to accept each other as we are, to embrace change if needed, and that we look out for our neighbours."

Lara smiled, "As a newcomer, I agree with your assessment of the *spirit* of Spirit Town.

Jon nodded, "As a policeman, I'm used to not being accepted into a community, but here, it's like I belong. Does anyone mind if I have a second bread roll?"

"Go for it, mate, I'm going to. We made sure there was enough for two each, though we know some of us eat more than others." Seamus reached for a second roll.

Izzie batted his hand away, "Ladies first, and yes I'm probably the only lady who'll eat a second roll, but a girl's got to keep her strength up."

"I don't know how you do it Izzie," Lara commented. "Eight hours in the shop and I'm ready for bed. You get what, four hours sleep a night?"

"Something like that. I run on adrenaline, caffeine and calories," she quipped piling her burger high with chicken and salad.

Chapter Thirty-Four

I let the banter of my friend's flow around me. My spider senses were trying to tell me something. "I'll be back in a minute," I said vaguely to the room in general. Spark jumped off Lexi's lap, one step in front as I opened the door to Grandma's room. A light glow emanated from the box on the bed. I opened the lid. The secret journal cover shone a vibrant deep red. It warmed under my touch.

Grandma's writing flowed, neatly, in old fashioned handwritten pencil. The words caught the light and shone brightly as I read them, creating an illusion that the words ran along the page, like a ripple across a stream. The secret journal appeared to be a collection of spells, providing details on how to manipulate the elements – water, air, earth, fire, and spirit. "I'm not sure that spell is the right term," I told Spark. He'd jumped up, curled up into a ball next to the journal, listening to me read with one eye open. "It's more like a list of instructions, which will come in handy." I stood, my knees creaking from kneeling. "Better get back, before they send a search party," I giggled, the directions for mastering elemental magic buzzing around in my head.

"Ah here she is, we were getting worried about you. They thought you may have fallen asleep, but I knew better," Izzie grinned.

"A cuppa anyone?" I pressed the button on the kettle, making sure the water level would cope with six mugs of coffee. "I decided to read some of Grandma's journal. It's given me ideas for what my show of power could be."

"And?" Izzie asked, "Also no coffee for me, I'd better head home." She pushed her chair back, "unless you're actually going to tell us what you're thinking."

"Not yet," I replied, "It's still percolating in my brain." I scooped a heaped teaspoon of coffee into the other mugs.

"None for me either, thanks Beth." Lexi rose from her chair.

"Then I guess I'll be bringing leftover dessert to you both tomorrow," I grinned, "As long as I leave some for Seamus as well," I giggled as a look of horror crossed his face, at the thought of missing out on seconds.

"I guess I could meet you both at the newspaper around 11am, to save you the trip to the station," Izzie conceded with a smile. "Thanks Seamus, Beth, come on Lexi, I'll walk you to your car."

I walked my two journalistic friends to their cars. "Thanks for coming. I'll see you tomorrow. Please be careful. I don't mean to scare you, but we know they're trying to annoy us, er, me, so please be careful." I remembered the earlier events of the day and added, "But try not to worry Lexi. I've placed a protection spell around the office, the council and here. It's worked so far." I reached into my pocket, finding the small piece of clear quartz. I handed it to Lexi. "Keep this with you, in your pocket, or your bra. It was Grandma's. It will keep you safe." Before she could say anything, or we all burst into tears, I hugged them both. Spark, who'd managed to get into Lexi's arms, extricated himself, landed lightly in my arms. They both promised to be extra vigilant as they hopped into their cars.

In the kitchen, Seamus served us each a bowl of dessert, orange poppyseed cake and custard, with blueberries. "I thought you'd appreciate the fruit," he grinned at me.

"I do, thank you," my voice caught in my throat, so I busied myself with my spoon, savouring the delicious blend of sugary dessert and slightly less sweet berries. Seamus's thoughtfulness made me smile. The four of us ate our desserts in silence.

Lara spoke first. "Do you need us to do anything tomorrow, before Friday's meeting?"

My heart warmed at her question. "Goodness, I've not thought in detail about Friday yet, at least not the practical side of it. The school will have the chairs set up; we pretty much just turn up. Lexi and Izzie have been working hard, getting people to think about how we can help the tenants, and there's Lily's proposal. I'll spend some time tomorrow reading and jotting down some notes."

"Do you have any idea of numbers you're expecting?" Jon asked. "Fred or I will be there, not both of us, in case we are needed elsewhere. I mean, if I were Max or Dean, I'd take the opportunity to cause mischief, either at the meeting or somewhere else."

I yawned and cupped my hand to my mouth, "Oops sorry, long day. Tomorrow morning I'll work out a plan and text you with a rough plan for Friday."

Lara glanced at Jon, "We should get going, do you want a hand cleaning up first?"

"Thanks, but it'll only take a few minutes, I can do it. I appreciate you guys always being here to help." I stacked the bowls next to the sink, Lara followed with the empty mugs.

The four of us crossed the hallway to the front door. Jon and Lara left together and hopped into Lara's car. "I can drop you back to the station if you need to check in on Fred," I heard her say as she closed the door.

"I'll be back early tomorrow morning; we can drive into work together." Seamus touched me gently on the arm, the action sent tingles down my spine.

"You can stay here tonight if you like," I spoke quietly, feeling every part of him standing so close.

"I could, but I need to check on the farm, have a shower and a change of clothes, my own clothes," he responded, just as quietly. I knew he sensed the growing attraction between us.

What I wanted to say was – *you can bring your clothes here and stay forever.* What I said instead was "Sounds fair enough. I can drive myself to work, if you need to catch up on farm stuff."

I stood in the doorway, refusing to shut and lock the door until he drove away, despite knowing he'd prefer if I'd been safely behind a locked door before he left. Would I ever let my guard down enough to share with him the depth of my feelings? Little sparks of electricity escaped through my fingertips. Rather than trying to calm myself, to keep my power at bay, I leant into my emotions. *It's not fair – that my parents died, before I returned, that my grandma died such a long time ago. How dare Max, Dean and others keep trying to ruin things!* I stomped my feet on the verandah, the wooden beams shaking under the force of my anger.

My familiar looked up and mewed at me. Instinct told me to place him inside, and without second guessing it, I tucked him in the screen door. Seconds later a large blackbird land on the verandah railing. In the moonlight, the bird's shiny sleek feather shone. His raucous caw echoed in the still evening air. "You're a message, aren't you? For me, I just wish I knew what you were trying to tell me." She cawed again, twice, and rose, her beating wings causing a breeze. I shuddered, out of anticipation, not fear.

Another yawn escaped my lips as I locked the front door. Spark shadowed me as I made sure all the doors and windows were secure. I'd plans to read the journal, figure out my plan to show strength and power, and wash up. Instead, I changed into my pyjamas, picked up my kitten and climbed into bed.

Chapter Thirty-Five

I woke in a sweat, more tangled in my blankets than normal. Spark had migrated to my pillow, patting my face until he pulled me out of nightmare. "Thanks, little guy." I closed my eyes, trying to remember what had caused the sweat. *Pat, pat, pat,* my familiar seemed insistent. "Okay, okay," I wiggled my bottom, making myself sit up so I didn't doze off.

With the impression that it wasn't just a dream, but a warning of some sort, I swung my legs over the side of my bed. Maybe a coffee would clear my fuzzy brain fog. "It's unusual that I slept for so long," I mused, noting it'd soon be 5am. Spark stared back at me, when he reached the threshold, making sure I'd planned to follow him.

As the kettle boiled, I decided to check on Buddy. While he nibbled the apple, I looked around the garden, something felt out of place. I slipped on the gumboots that sat beside the door, shaking them first, in case any spiders had decided to take up residence. The path wasn't too slippery, still, I took slow deliberate steps, lest my boots slip, as they had previously. I ran my hands along the rows of fragrant bushes I'd help Grandma plant either side of the path Dad paved.

Luckily, I saw the thing on the ground before I tripped on it. I hesitated, not knowing whether to pick it up. I'd not left any tools outside, and I'd no reason to have used a screwdriver in the garden. Spark's little nose checked out the item on the ground. "Should I get a freezer bag, and pick it up in that?" He plonked his bottom on the paver stone in front of the offending object, indicating he'd guard it while I found something appropriate to pop it into until I could decide what to do with it.

Turning the plastic bag inside out, I picked the tool up by the metal end, lest the black handle have any identifying fingerprints. "Come on Spark," I tracked the rest of the path to the little wooden gate in the fence at the end of our block. Tucked in between bushes and trees my grandma and parents planted, I couldn't recall a time we'd used the gate, though it must have been there for a reason. I'd found it unlocked a couple of times, but figured it was just people causing mischief. I wiggled the lock. It didn't appear to have been tampered with. "I guess an intruder could've jumped one of the side fences, though why I don't know." I sighed, just one more thing to figure out. "Another reason to show my strength."

I jumped in the shower while the kettle boiled, leaving Spark with Buddy, knowing that he'd stay with his friend. Seamus walked through the front door as I exited the bathroom, luckily with clothes on. "Morning." I smiled, my lifelong friend looked particularly handsome in a deep blue shirt, with his dark denim jeans.

The blush on my cheeks, as I remembered he could read my mind didn't go un-noticed. "Morning to you too," he smiled. "I like your purple blouse, is it new?"

"A few years old, not sure if I've worn it for a while, I found it tucked behind some dresses." It'd fallen off its hanger, I wasn't sure if it needed an iron, but it appears I got away with it, making a point of buying clothes that didn't need ironing. "I've just boiled the kettle, if you'd like a cuppa."

"I'll never say no to a cuppa. What's this?" he pointed to the bag lying on the kitchen bench.

"I found the tool on the back path, it's a little silly, but I picked it up by the bag, in case it's got prints on it." I poured water into our two favourite mugs. Neither had suffered even a crack or a chink in their colours over the last twenty years. We chose them for their bright colours and the silly faces painted on them.

Seamus eyed me, a solemn look, as he drank from the bright orange mug. "Jeez Beth, I go home for one night and someone tries to break in? Have you checked all the windows and doors?" He strode to the back door, noticing Spark on the other side, still visiting with Buddy.

Spark entered the house as Seamus opened the door, wandering over to his water bowl as the door lock was secured with its key. "It was next, after my cuppa, and before I left for work." Seamus was already off down the hallway opening doors, and rattling window locks. Spark glanced up from his bowl. "I'm sure you'll be safe here today, unless you want to go to Lexi's." Before I'd finished speaking, my kitten had pounced on my bare feet, tickling them with his tiny claws. "Hehehe, that tickles."

"Are you planning to go to work barefoot today?" Seamus raised an eyebrow as he returned to the kitchen,

"Impatient much?" I furrowed my brows together, "Oh and we're taking Spark to Lexi on the way to work," I ducked into my room, returning a few seconds later with socks and boots, expecting a grumble about using Lexi as a kitten sitter.

He surprised me. "Not a bad idea. I have another one, I have to be at the farm around lunchtime, so I was hoping I could convince you to have breakfast at Evie's and dinner here, if that's okay?"

I was okay Seamus's day revolving around food, his fast metabolism caused him dizzy spells if he didn't eat often enough. "I suppose that's fair, except you don't have to eat dinner with me here, unless you want to..." my voice faltered, not wanting to sound like I wanted him to stay, nor did I want to sound like I didn't. Were all relationships such hard work?

"Right, well, that's that then, come on." Seamus turned away quickly, but not before I noticed a reddening of his cheeks. I scooped up

Spark, my laptop bag, which luckily, I'd packed earlier and locked the front door.

Chapter Thirty-Six

Lexi snuggled Spark, waving me away, "I'm sure Seamus is starving, Spark and I will be fine."

Seamus held up a plastic shopping bag. "Aren't you forgetting something? It's lucky I remembered this morning."

I peeked in the bag, "Thanks! It would be a little difficult to have morning tea later, if you'd forgotten as well." I skipped to the little kitchenette, putting the bag with the cakes straight into the fridge. "Okay, let's get going, I'm looking forward to our morning tea later." I patted Spark as he wrapped himself around Lexi's feet.

Kids, parents, contractors, professionals, I'd become accustomed to how busy Evie's café could be. Could I get used to having a meal here, most days? Probably, with the right company. In the last few months, I'd made many small changes, and I was not normally comfortable with change. Today I stepped a little more lightly, my energy buzzing more contentedly. If I wasn't careful, I'd end up feeling like I'd come home, like I had a place here. I caught my friend looking at me. "Coffee and a big breakfast wrap for you, a coffee and a bowl of fruit for me." My plan was to beat him to ordering so I could pay for once.

A group of elves in blue and green ran through from the kitchen, each carrying baskets filled with bread rolls. They nimbly raced each other, zigzagging around other patrons, disappearing through the front door. A flurry of fairies waving their wands followed a few seconds later. At the wifi desk, a young woman's coffee floated just above the bench, making it a little tricky for the well-dressed woman trying to finish it.

Excited squeals emanated from the kid's corner. I couldn't see exactly what was moving on the shelves, but the children were enthralled. Two young mothers sat crossed legged on the floor watching their youngsters. Even the couple of older people sharing a plate of pancakes, with a milkshake each, were giggling like teens.

Since I managed to order before Seamus opened his mouth, he chose a seat right in the middle of the café. Even that didn't throw me this morning. All thoughts of my weird nightmare vanished. My bowl of fruit with its bananas, mango and berries beat the breakfast wrap hands down. "I'm loving this fresh fruit, a great energy boost for the day ahead."

Taking a huge bite of his wrap, he glanced around the café. "Is it just me, or does everything feel lighter today?"

"I was just thinking the same thing," I murmured, scraping the last few berries from the bottom of the bowl. I wasn't sure if I should mention the noticeable absence of our esteemed ex-mayor and his crony, or whether that would jinx the good vibes. I decided to stay quietly optimistic that maybe they'd moved on to create havoc in another location.

Bessie floated over to the table, her pink and white pinafore hovering just above the tiled floor. "Can I get you anything else?" she asked beaming.

I placed my mug in my bowl. "I'm good thanks. Just the perfect amount of food to start my day," I smiled at Evie's mother.

The door swung open, as Finn and Maeve entered the café, dressed as dramatically as when I'd visited their shop with Lara. They both nodded curtly as I said *good morning* on our way through the door. "Cheery lot," Seamus commented with a chuckle. As we moved further from the café, Seamus ventured the question I'd been waiting for, "Any plans on how you're going to demonstrate your strength and magic ability? I know it's not a part of your life you're normally comfortable with."

"A few ideas are forming in my mind, mainly to do with elemental magic," was all I'd say. Not because I didn't want to tell him, but the vague idea of using the elements, the way Grandma described in her journal was as far as my planning went.

"Hmm, tonight we can work it out together," I loved my best friend for his support but we both knew it was something I had to work out for myself. I held the door open, after punching in the four-digit pin code. "This is easier than fiddling around for a key," I acknowledged. "As long as I don't forget the code."

"Uhuh," was all he'd say. "I mightn't see you until after work. Are you happy for me to organise dinner? If you want to get dessert though, I wouldn't mind."

I gave him the thumbs up sign as I pushed open the door to my office. I rummaged in the fridge; thankful I'd shoved a twelve pack of water bottles in there last week. Inhaling, holding my breath, and exhaling, I felt a tingling in that patch of skin on my forehead often referred to as my third eye. I closed my other eyes and zoned in on the image of me, sitting with Grandma, on a wooden seat that used to sit in the back garden. The memory grew clearer, as if it'd occurred a few days ago. Tears started running along my cheeks.

How does it work Grandma? five-year-old me asked.

Magic, she replied.

That doesn't make sense, even then I'd preferred logic over what I couldn't see or understand.

When you grow older, you'll come into your powers, the ability to see things, help people, know things, and change situations for the better. Until then, and always, you have elemental magic.

What does mental magic mean?

Grandma waved her hand, muttered a few words I didn't understand, and a little wind blew a cloud in front of us. She wiggled her fingers, and the cloud rained on my feet. Five-year-old me giggled. Then Grandma moved her feet, and in the empty garden bed in front of her, flowers stretched up through the dry earth. A click of her fingers and a fire burnt the flowers back into nothingness.

I gasped, as did mini me. I didn't need to continue to watch to remember what happened next. I'd clicked my fingers, causing a fire to start in the compost bin, panicked, waved my arms and a dark grey cloud had dumped enough snow on half of Spirit Town that the emergency services had to be called. Grandma explained away the flowers that sprung up throughout backyard as early spring planting, though I suspected my parents knew the truth. That may have been why they forbade Grandma to teach me any more of the old ways.

Holding my hands out in front of me, I stared at them. I saw nothing particularly unusual about them. A few scratches from Spark's claws, my fingernails could do with a trim, and there was the odd freckle on the back of my not very tanned hand. Turning them over, I wasn't sure what the lines on my hands told me about my future, or my past. No rings, polish or other adornments. A couple of veins pulsed on the backs of my hands. Did these hands create that mess, as a five-year-old? And could these old, more mature hands, create such things now? In a more controlled, adult logical way.

A little zap of electricity from the middle finger on my right hand suggested that yes it was possible. I moved each finger up and down, ever so slightly, angling them away from my laptop. A few more zaps later, I figured it could be a little dangerous to pursue the activity in a confined space.

My emails blinked, beckoning for me to attend to my mayoral duties. Aware that in a little under twenty-four hours I'd be chairing the town meeting, I read all the emails, responding to those I could, flagging the others that needed further investigation. I grabbed the documents relevant to the meeting, and compiled a running sheet – ordering the agenda of the meeting. I emailed it to my fellow councillors, Lexi and Izzie, for any suggestions.

Aware my nerves were creating waves of nervous energy, I stood, stretched and went for a walk. A customer enquiry was occupying Mikayla. I waved, figuring I'd talk to her after my morning tea, and left the building. Rather than turning left, the quickest way to the newspaper office, I turned right and soon found myself in the open space at the entry to our local park. In a daze, I moved past the fragrant garden, and the playground area, into the more secluded natives section.

Pre-occupied with thoughts of elemental magic, I became aware of my fingers. As if a force deep inside were urging them on, my digits moved slowly, up and down, up and down, weaving a story, calling to the elements. Intuitively knowing no one could see me, I focused on the air around me, how it whispered among the leaves. A deep breath in. As I released my own air, twined with my energy, did I imagine it, or did the wind whip up a pile of leaves and branches mulched under the shrubs? I tried again, focusing on a particularly small bush with larger leaves. *Holy Cow!* If I'd not seen it with my own eyes, not one would've convinced me that my energy could create such a whoosh of air.

With my fingers tingling, I imagined water, sprinkling gently down from a cloud, nourishing the soil around the plant. My eyes blinked rapidly as I realised, I'd created the little cloud and the rain tumbling from it. I held out my fingers, hoping to catch a drop, as proof of my own ability. I marvelled at the droplet of moisture on my fingertip. In my mind I saw the daisies Grandma loved so much dainty pink and white, and bang – in the soil still damp from my rain, little bits of green sprang forth. As the green unfurled, flower buds formed that turned into flowers in front of my eyes.

Buoyed by my initial success, *it's easier than it looks,* I decided to try fire. Appreciating the danger of creating a flame in such combustible surroundings I moved towards the metal garbage bin at the edge of the picnic area. I wasn't keen on burning the plastics and wrappers, lest they emitted a harmful odour. I grabbed a couple of handfuls of leaves, piling them on top of the normal rubbish. I let the heat of my emotions run down to my fingertips, pointing them at the bin. As a few wisps of smoke wafted up out of the bin I panicked. I didn't want the fire to get out of hand. I waved my arms in front of me, and a wave of water splashed into the rubbish bin, extinguishing the leaf litter. I jumped, a little jittery, looking around to make sure no one had noticed my antics. Assured that no one saw me, and pleased with my use of elemental magic, I hurried to the newspaper office.

Chapter Thirty-Seven

Lexi opened the door with a smile, and a plate of lamingtons. "There you are," she beamed. Spark echoed her sentiments, wrapping his little furry body around my ankles. "Izzie messaged that she'll be here in a few minutes."

I joined Lexi in the conference room where two plates of cakes, the lamingtons and leftover orange poppyseed cake, sat at one end of the long table. Three cups of peppermint tea sat steeping in cups in front of three chairs.

"Amazing! Just what I needed, thanks so much Lexi," I gave my work colleague a quick hug. As I plonked my backside on the chair my body buzzed, energised and drained simultaneously. "How are things going here?" I noticed a pile of manilla folders at the other end of the table.

She eyed the folders, "I've been doing research, finding whatever information I can on those who've been exiled over the years. Only a few were exiled, not nearly as many as I thought. Not all the residents who used their magic the wrong way were punished with exile. The council only took such drastic action if the perpetrator exhibited wilful intent to harm others. I'd no idea that so many people experimented with their magic. In many instances their powers caused a fuss but they didn't mean any harm. The magic council were lenient in many cases. Only hardened criminal types who showed no remorse were told to leave."

Before I could comment the front door banged open. "Is this a private party or can anyone join in?" Izzie's dulcet tones announced her arrival. She dropped a box of chocolates on the table. "For Lexi, for being awesome," she said with a flourish and a bow. "Before I forget, Lexi, I found some people you might want to talk to, I'll email their details." Izzie's expression told me she was up to something, there was always another layer of facts when she had her nose on the trail of a story.

I sat, and passed the plate of lamingtons to Izzie, after taking one and placing it on my plate. "If you're talking about the 'real' history of the Spirit Town exiles, I support you one hundred percent. It doesn't matter if you uncover that my family were in the right or wrong, whether they were murdered or arranged such things, I'm keen to know the truth."

Izzie and Lexi exchanged a look, "Good, because Lexi made an excellent point, that we, collectively, need to understand the history, to understand what's going on now." Izzie pulled a pile of newspaper clippings from her bag. "Don't ask me how, because a good reporter will never reveal her sources, but I collected these years ago. I found them when I was decluttering." Izzie moved to the city, initially to university and then to pursue a high-flying journalistic career, had returned to Spirit Town when her mum became sick.

I sipped my tea, the peppermint steam invigorating my senses. After my attempt at elemental magic, I needed it. "I'll happily devour all information you can find. I'd rather be informed than get caught out. I do have one question," I put my cup down, guilty at even bringing it up. "How do you know the information is real, not manipulated in some way? I mean we've seen how the truth around here gets bent especially ifs about something magical."

"You're not the only one with intuition," Izzie said haughtily. "I've developed a knack for being able to *see* the truth. Let's just say I can peg a falsehood a kilometre away."

"Good to know," I smiled, with no idea of why I blushed...well maybe some idea...if Izzie could tell the truth from a well-meant fib, I should probably come clean about my feelings for Seamus one day soon. I watched my friends while I ate my lamington. "Did you get a chance to read my email? What did I miss in terms of tomorrow's meeting?" I listened, as they both added some ideas, which would be useful. "I'd love it if you could get me a rough figure, how many have been exiled from Spirit Town over say fifty years? If you can't, that's totally fine, I know you're both busy."

"I'll do my best," Lexi passed me a piece of cake. I hesitated, having already eaten a couple of lamingtons, but the spell casting left me more drained than I thought. "Are we allowed to ask about the show of strength, do you have any idea what you might do?"

"Good question. I tested my powers earlier, and it turns out I remember some of the skills Grandma taught me. I'm still a little fuzzy on the details."

Izzie put down her cup or tea, "You often sell yourself short, I mean, you might remember what your grandma taught you, or you might just know, that ability is deep within you. From my reading, even a powered person with no training at all can conjure up an elephant or a mouse. You're from this long magical line of kick-ass women. I imagine you could easily show us something spectacular."

I got the impression Izzie had the right concept of how it worked. "Okay, so what do you suggest. I can manipulate air, water, earth, fire, plants and things. What can I do, that's a show of my strength but won't harm anyone or the town?"

We all ate our cakes in silence, mulling over the problem. "Oh, I know!" Lexi jumped up, nearly knocking Spark from where he'd crawled onto my lap, purring contentedly. She scooped him up, nuzzled his fur, and returned him to my lap where he settled back in. Suddenly self-conscious, she continued in a quieter tone, "Do you think you could create a new row of shops, or something, on the Wynyard Street site?" She hesitated, glancing at me, then Izzie. "I mean, that's harnessing the elements, and depending on what materials you use, it's all that and more."

"Lexi, you're brilliant." I stood up, gently removing Spark first, and hugged her.

"Playing devil's advocate, what if someone moans that you're not allowing contractors to bid for the work if you create it all in one big poof of smoke?" Izzie asked in her best reporter voice.

"What about if I create the shell, we still need contractors to fit it all out. In an environmentally sound way." I ad-libbed, as my heart leapt in my chest, indicating I was on the right track. "Do we need to talk about anything else?" The idea grew in my head, forming a clear picture of what I'd create on the site. I could provide options for employment, not just for the current tenants but others as well. "It's just, you've given me such a great idea, I want to get organised."

"Whoa, hang on," Izzie raised her hand. "How are you going to do it? It can't just appear overnight, no one will know you created it. You'll have to do it in front of a large crowd, preferably Max and Dean as well."

Izzie was right. "And it should be after the town meeting," I acknowledged.

"Isn't the school hall only a short walk from the site? How about straight after, invite everyone to join you?" Lexi suggested.

I clapped my hands together. "Will that work?" I asked, nerves racing around my body.

"I don't see why not," Izzie tapped the keypad on her mobile, "Making myself a note," she explained. She pointed at me. "You have to make sure the other councillors are on side, it's no good going to all the trouble to plan this and have them throw you out, again." Her smile indicated she was behind me all the way. She turned to Lexi, "Once Beth messages us that council approves, you can update social media, and I'll talk about it on the radio. We can make it vague and intriguing enough that people will turn out in droves," She drained her cup, picked up another couple of lamingtons, "for later," and waved as she headed out the door.

"It always feels like a hurricane, spending time with Izzie," Lexi commented.

"A positive hurricane," I concurred.

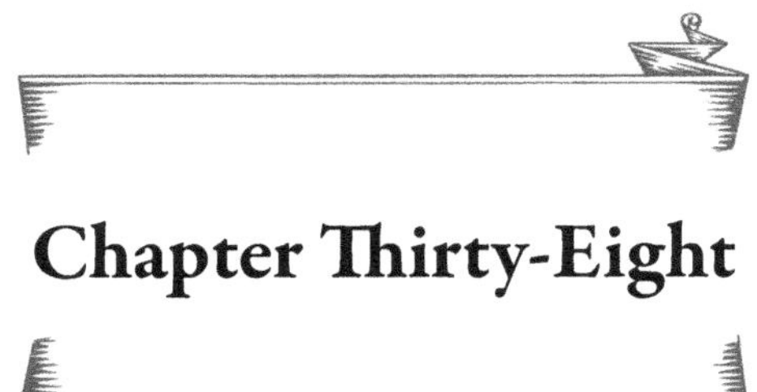

Chapter Thirty-Eight

I surveyed the councillors seated around the table. "I appreciate you all turning up to an impromptu meeting, you're all busy with projects. I just wanted to make sure we're on the same page for tomorrow morning's meeting. I'd like the focus to be what we, as a community can do to assist the Wynyard Street tenants. I'm expecting questions levelled at me, as mayor. I'm planning to answer all those, giving as much detail as I can at the time, rather than saying I'll get back to them later."

Heads nodded.

"Do we have an indication of numbers?" Jamie asked.

"A rough guesstimate is a couple of hundred," I'd completed a quick tally of the responses received by myself, Mikayla, Lexi and Izzie. "Last time we met we briefly discussed inviting exiled members to return," I paused as a couple of indistinct grumbles rippled around the table. "The number of exiles is way smaller than we thought. I'll get that exact number to you asap. I want to pose an idea given to me by one of our residents. It was suggested that if I demonstrated a show of my own magical strength, it may stop the others from continuing to cause trouble locally. I didn't embrace the idea at first, as I'm not keen to cause any damage myself. Then I realised a show of strength doesn't have to be destructive." I made a point of staring each person directly in the eyes, seeing their reaction and assuring them of my intent. Seamus's eyes told me he knew and supported my next words. "I propose creating a shell of the new shopping complex on the Wynyard Street site, including a park and children's playground. We'd still need to engage local contractors for the fit out, supporting Spirit Town businesses." I crossed my fingers together in my lap, waiting for comments.

Kim, normally the quietest and the only other female spoke first. "I've noticed more magic around town, over the last few days. I don't know what's happening to cause it. If it has anything to do with Dean or Max, then a demonstration of how we can use magic to help others...especially by our mayor, I'd consider a positive action."

"What does Agnes and the magic council say?" Jamie sounded optimistic, rather than the droll, negative person he'd been on other occasions.

"Agnes suggested it, and the magic council supports the idea." I'd received a text as I'd left the newspaper, confirming this.

Glen leant forward, "Don't take this the wrong way, but can you do it? Have you practiced somewhere or are you expecting to get there tomorrow and hope it works?"

I flashed a smile at Glen, buoyed by the mainly positive comments of my colleagues. "I'd the same thought, and I've practiced a little, and will do some more later on, the last thing I want to do is create more problems." Greg fidgeted in his chair; it was clear he wanted to say something. "You can say or ask anything, I won't be offended." I told the group, rather than singling him out. "We have to all trust each other and honesty is a huge part of that."

Greg cleared his throat. "Public liability, insurance, that sort of thing, in case, well, you know, something goes wrong on site, not that I think it will, but..." his voice trailed off, as he looked around the table for support. All eyes turned to me.

I scribbled a note. "Thanks, that's a very good point. I've the highest level of insurance on the site; I know that because I've spoken to the company after the fire. They understand the special circumstances of Spirit Town and some of its residents. I'll contact them shortly to have a chat. It would be Beth the person, not the mayoral office who'd wear any costs," I assured them.

Seamus still hadn't spoken. I knew he'd let the others go first. He caught my eye, looked at the others and asked, "In a practical sense, is there anything you need us to do?"

"At the meeting, I'd appreciate it if you could mingle, talk to anyone who comes along for chat. I've sent through the updated list of questions, and the final agenda. Please review it, because there's time to update it if we need to." I sipped water from my bottle. "I think that covers everything regards tomorrow. Does anyone have any questions, or any other business?"

There wasn't. As we filed out of the conference room, I found Mikayla. "Do you have a few minutes?"

She smiled, "Yes, I've an appointment at 3pm, but I'm all yours for ten minutes."

"Firstly, thanks for all your help. I've sent you an email, so you know the agenda for tomorrow. I'll make sure to update you if there are any last-minute changes. In the meantime, any questions, issues, thoughts etc, please text or email. It doesn't matter what time, I'll answer. My plan is to come here early tomorrow morning, before heading to the school."

Mikayla's pen wrote neat lines across her notepad. "Do you want me to take minutes of the meeting?"

I smiled, "That would be brilliant, thanks."

The door to my office being open should've set off alarm bells. Too preoccupied with my plans for the following morning and ticking off my to do list in my head I almost ran into the visitor. The whoosh of our energies pushing against each other jolted me to attention. *Jacob!*

"Cousin," the man standing just inside my door stood half a head taller than me. With brown work boots, old blue jeans, and a checkered shirt, he could've been any of the farmers who lived around Spirit Town. His short dark hair, and dark eyes, were broody, more than I remembered the only other time I'd met him in person. Looking not un-like Dean, I realised, shuddering at the thought I might be related to Dean as well. Jacob's tone was difficult to identify. My instinct told me he wasn't happy.

"Jacob. Good to see you, would you like a cup of tea, or a glass of water?" I motioned for him to sit down.

He shook his head. "Can't stay. Wanted to warn you, or rather Dean wanted me to warn you, not to go ahead with your research. It won't help you, knowing the details of the people your family exiled." As he spoke, a lightbulb went off in my head. Could there be informa-tion at home that'd tell me what I wanted to know?

"And why is that? I do wish you'd sit down, so we could talk prop-erly." I wasn't fearful, just exasperated. I knew Jacob could be cagey, only revealing snippets of information, but to threaten me on behalf of Dean? I didn't have the time or energy to be playing these games. "Are you and Dean going to attend the meeting tomorrow morning? I'd like you to, if that means anything." Did I sound too desperate? Genuine?

"Just, stop, looking for answers. Don't make the same mistakes as the rest of your family." Without another word, he turned on his heel and left my office. I heard the outer door slam, before I'd formulated any words to plead my case.

"A family reunion?" Seamus spoke softly, so as not to scare me, as he walked in from outside. "Not a particularly friendly chap, I tried to say hi, but he totally ignored me."

"I wouldn't take it personally. He only came to warn me, on Dean's behalf," I shook my head, to clear the residue anxiety left by Jacob's words. "How's your day going?"

"Busy. I'm just checking in to see if you're still okay for dinner at yours. Unless you're too busy prepping for tomorrow."

Every part of my body wanted to yell *yes please come over and stay forever ...* and *... no thanks, I'm fine.* Neither response would do. I should learn from my mistakes. We were more than friends, we both felt it. The time had come for honesty. "That would be very nice." I didn't care that my cheeks burned brighter than a tomato. "I'd like to hear about your day, and I'd like some help with my plans for tomorrow."

Seamus grinned. The type of genuine, goofy grin, he gave me when I offered to take him to the café, or when we used to spend the weekend together, as teens, exploring the town, eating something in each of the cafes and bakeries. "Do you mind Chinese for dinner? You can choose the dessert, even fruit if you like. And is 6pm too late? It's just I've got to do a few things first."

"I'll pick up dessert and some other treats as well," my energy buzzed, Seamus's too. "It doesn't matter if you're late. Bring a change of clothes too if you like," I couldn't believe I'd said it out loud.

Neither could Seamus, his grew cheeks as red as tomatoes. "Er, um, okay, well, I'll see you later." For the second time in less than an hour, a man walked out of my office.

The question that spun around in my brain wasn't about the town meeting tomorrow, or how I could show my strength. Instead of thinking about identifying the names of the people my family exiled from Spirit Town, I had one thought. *Would I have the courage to tell Seamus how I really felt?*

Chapter Thirty-Nine

The possibility that my power could be useful, wasn't something I'd ever considered. I debated whether to try to find the information in the ledgers my family kept through paranormal means. "Could I wave my hands over the rows of books, making the book with the answers fall out of the shelf, open at the right page?" I asked Spark.

My familiar walked over to the shelf in Grandma's wardrobe where the ledgers she kept were stored. "Even if I manage it, where do I start to look for the more up to date information? Dad used computers and thumb drives, but what about Mum?" I wish I knew the magical rules and whether familiars knew answers about people they'd not met.

Spark responded by sitting in front of the shelves. "Okay, do you want to move a little, I'm not sure if this'll work." I thought about the answers I sought, the number of, and names of the people who'd been exiled over the last hundred years, by my ancestors. Contact details would be perfect, but I doubted that additional information would be available.

I focused my mind to picture my grandma's handwriting, revealing to me the answers I sought. I channelled my energy into my hands and my fingers. I pictured Grandma and my parents, writing the details in their ledgers. My fingers pulsed. I let the intensity build up until whoosh – I waved my hand across in front of the books.

Nothing moved. I sighed, admonishing myself for thinking I could do it. My bottom lip trembled as I began to turn away. My kitten mewed and I jumped, as a book on the middle shelf propelled itself out of the wardrobe and onto the floor. It flew open, the covers banging as they touched the floor on either side. I watched the pages flip from front to back, until they stopped. Fingers crossed I crouched down over the volume and read the words on the open page.

The exiled few – 1901 – 2023

I recognised Grandma's handwriting, though she passed in 1997. I'd met her ghost – that she could write in the journal didn't surprise me. The surprise was that only five names were listed. *Jacob Harriott, Dean Collier, Clara O'Reily, Ethel Barnaby, and Jordan Graham.* Underneath the names I found a numerical reference penned in my mother's neat handwriting. *1208.*

The numbers could have many meanings. My intuition told me I needed to find a modern-day reference. Not having found my parents' computer anywhere in the house hadn't phased me too much. Dad's school office contained one, and maybe they didn't own one at home, though the few messages I'd received from them since they passed had been via emails, computer printed pages, and a thumb drive.

Spark mewed. I returned the book to its home, after taking a photograph of the page. He stared at the coat hanger where the patchwork gown hung. I slipped the garment over my underclothes, not surprised when it fitted perfectly, like it'd been made for me. I slipped my hands into the pockets which hung just off my waist. In one, a little silver velvet pouch held a gold ring, a piece of clear quartz and a dried daisy tucked into a golden locket. The other held a piece of cream coloured parchment paper. I turned it over a couple of times, but found no markings, messages, letters or numbers.

"Let's try something." I whispered to Spark, placing the piece of paper onto Grandma's bed. I let the heat of my energy pool in the palm of my hand. As my skin pulsed, I waved my palm over the parchment.

1208 Beth

Those numbers again, and my name. The numbers triggered something in my brain, though I couldn't quite put my finger on its significance. I closed my eyes. In the scene tucked in behind my eyelids, I was playing hide and seek with Grandma. I crouched in the back of my wardrobe, under my thick woollen jacket that used to be itchy when I wore it. I waited for ages before she found me.

A gentle breeze whipped around me. Neither hot nor cold, it beckoned me to follow. Feeling a little like a goddess in the flowing magical gown, I moved along in the wind as it led me to my room, opening the door to my wardrobe.

I heard myself take in a sharp breath as I realised that same itchy coat hung at the end of my clothes, squashed by the other coats I wore as I got older, and taller.

Gently moving the coats to one side I rubbed my hand along the wooden inside of the cupboard. My skin caught on rough marks scratched into the wood. I took the torch from my bedside table and shone it on the wall. Crudely etched in the wall were the numbers 1208.

Pushing the clothes as far as I could to my right, I moved into the space. A little door, carved into the wall, became clear the closer I moved towards it. A hole, that could be mistaken for a knot in the wood, no bigger than my little finger appeared to be the only way in. I stuck my little finger in the hole and the door swung open. Inside sat a laptop. Not as new as mine, I realised as I lifted it out of its hiding place.

A small material pouch, taped to the front of the machine, contained a charging cord.

"Wow…" I heard Seamus, as if I were far away. in a cloud, so focused on the items in my hands.

I turned to greet him with a huge smile, "Hi."

He held up a heavy paper bag. The Chinese food smelt amazing. "I almost hate to mention it, but I brought dinner," He eyed my dress, "would you like to change into something…less formal…"

"Sure," I giggled at how uncomfortable he looked. "There are plates, spoons, forks, and glasses in the kitchen, on the table. There's some ginger beer in the fridge. I'll be right there." I changed out of the gown, hanging it on a hanger from my wardrobe so it didn't crease, replacing the gown with my pink unicorn pyjamas.

"That's certainly a change," Seamus had two full plates and glasses ready by the time I met him in the kitchen. I placed the laptop and its charger on the kitchen bench, plugging it into the power to charge. "Back to normal then." He laughed at the look on my face, a mix between exasperation and being pleased to see him "I'm guessing the only thing you've eaten since breakfast is cake for morning tea, so please, eat." He nodded at my plate, heaped high with rice and three of our favourite Chinese dishes.

I nodded. We ate in silence. Eventually I could take it no longer. I wanted to talk to Seamus about what I found, and about the meeting tomorrow, and how I felt. Instead, I blurted out, "Did everything go okay at the farm?" Seamus's parents were currently on an extended around the world cruise, leaving Seamus to run the farm. He'd employed a manager and other farm hands. Mostly, it ran smoothly, but occasionally he needed to spend time there, to ensure it kept running smoothly.

"Rob wanted to talk to me about a new initiative, to do with farming alpacas. He's been talking to other local farmers, and some interstate, and has some great ideas for the farm. We met with some mates who already farm them. It's exciting." Never for one moment had Seamus bemoaned the fact he'd been left with the management of the farm, even though he had his two local businesses to run. Not to mention he'd stepped up for the stint on council, purely to support me.

I tried to read his mind, not something I often tried on purpose. Mostly the images just arrived in my head, like a soundtrack or a movie reel. "Do you regret signing up to council? Not that I'm suggesting you only did so to support me, that would be big headed of me, but do you wish you had more time for the farm, or the shops for that matter?"

He sat back in his chair, and crossed his arms, uncrossing them almost immediately. "I love helping people, being a part of our community. It brings a whole new energy, opportunities and experiences. Plus, you may have forgotten, you were away for twenty years, during which time I was intimately involved with the farm and the businesses." I caught the inflection, the hidden meaning and hurt behind the words.

Should I say out loud the feelings there were getting increasingly difficult to hold within? Spark moved out from under my feet, stepping daintily over to Seamus's chair. The butterflies in my stomach threatened to unsettle the satay and sweet and sour I'd just eaten. I swallowed, a little too loudly.

"I didn't mean anything by that comment," he looked uncomfortable, as if his meal had also decided to squirm in his stomach.

I took a breath, exhaling through my mouth. "It's not that..." the words caught in my throat. No matter how hard I tried, no words came. I decided to clear the table, piling the plates in the sink for later. I filled the kettle, turning it on for something to do, more than because I wanted a cuppa.

Seamus stood. "Suddenly I don't feel like dessert, maybe I should go."

He had totally the wrong idea. Why now did his ability to read me suddenly fail? Like my voice, which had decided to go on the fritz. I heard him, sigh, his footsteps headed slowly toward the front door. Had he brought a change of clothes, intending to stay the night, as I'd suggested earlier? The sound of the opening door turned on a switch somewhere deep inside. Unlocking a gate I'd shut long ago.

"Wait," my voice little more than a whisper, I crossed the space in a heartbeat. "Don't go..."

My oldest friend, the man I loved more than anyone else on this earth froze in place. He half turned; I saw that he had a small backpack in his hand. A vulnerable look in his eyes as tears gathered in the corners of his, as in mine. I took a couple of steps closer, reaching over and shutting the front door. "I was wrong," I hoped he read my thoughts, so I didn't have to say any more, lest I read the situation incorrectly.

A tiny smile played on his lips, "Really? When?"

Fine, he wanted me to say it out loud. "When I first returned and I said that we couldn't be more than friends, that it'd distract us too much from the businesses we were focusing on. Then we joined the council..."

His smile grew a little, "And now?"

If my heart beat any faster, I feared it would burst out of my chest. "Now I can't imagine going a day without seeing you, spending time with you..." I forced the words that caught in my throat to make their way into the world. I refused to let my brain think about what would happen if he disagreed with me. After all, that conversation happened months ago. He mightn't still feel the same way.

This time his ability to read my thoughts was spot on. "I've always loved you, since we were kids. The years, the distance, you telling me we had to focus on work, nothing will ever change that. I can handle being best friends, if that's all..." His voice filled with emotion, sounded husky, like he was also struggling with his words. "Are you saying that's changed?"

I wanted to reach out and touch him, but I hesitated. "We'll always be best friends. I'm scared if we open up to something more...what if I get it wrong...I don't ever want to hurt you..."

"You left abruptly, twenty years ago, and we're still...us. I'm willing to give it a try, if you are. As slowly as you need." He took a tentative step closer to where I seemed frozen in place, his backpack slipping out of his fingers, dropping to the floor with a soft thud.

Chapter Forty

It's Friday. My first thought as I opened my eye. A second thought quickly replaced it. *Seamus.* Spark snuggled into the small space between us, stirred as I wiggled to try and see the time without waking anyone.

"Coffee please, if you're getting up," mumbled my guest, a smile dancing across his face as he opened his eyes. He looked adorable, with his dark brown hair, all mussed up. As he moved on the bed, I saw his naked shoulders, and felt self-conscious, though he'd seen me in a singlet and shorts pyjamas before, a long time ago.

"It's early," I countered, knowing full well that while farmers were generally early risers, he wasn't all that keen with a 5am start to the day.

He sat up, rubbing the sleep from his eyes. "True, but it's a big day, and we got distracted last night, there's probably stuff you need to prepare, before the meeting."

"That's right, the meeting! There are things you need to know, to see, before the meeting. I meant to tell you last night, but we got distracted." I jumped out of bed. "I'll put the kettle on, have a quick shower, feed the animals, then I need to show you something."

Seamus climbed more sedately out of bed, lifting Spark to the ground first. He placed his hand on my arm. I felt the heat of his body on my skin. "Whoa, hold on. I can get the kettle going, and feed Spark and Buddy."

I stared into his eyes, the electric energy between us almost palpable. "Okay, thanks."

Too distracted to stand still for long enough for the shower water to heat up, I settled for a quick cold-water wash. I pulled on my black pants suit and red shirt, getting dressed in record time.

"I see you found your dad's computer," Seamus pointed his thumb at the laptop on the bench. I must've looked puzzled because he added, "There's a sticker on the back, it's a code."

I read the sticker. 1208

"Okay smarty pants, what does the code mean?"

"Really?" Seamus placed two mugs of steaming hot coffee on the table. "You don't recognise your date of birth?"

"My what?" I stared at the sticker. "Oh, of course it is." I didn't care that my cheeks flushed that he'd remembered my birthday after all these years. I recovered quickly. We didn't have much time to prepare for the meeting. "I suppose you know the password."

Seamus looked sheepish. "Am I in trouble if I say yes?" he pressed the button, firing up my dad's laptop.

"Not at all." I opened my phone, showing him the photo I'd taken yesterday. "From Grandma's journal. I'm pretty sure the laptop will have more information." I stood behind Seamus, watching the screen as the laptop home screen appeared. The flashing icon blinked, asking for a password. Seamus typed in 1208Beth and immediately the screen changed. I was staring at a photo of Seamus and I with my parents, shortly before we graduated.

A lump formed in my throat. Seamus looked up at me, "Are you okay?"

I nodded. I'd missed so many years with them all. I couldn't change that now. "I'm ready to move forward, I'm just a little sad, at, missing out on so much. What can we find that's useful?" I dragged my chair over and picked up my mug.

As Seamus clicked on icons, he asked, "Have you thought more about your show of power? Are you worried, or do you need some help preparing?" He pointed to my shirt. "What about wearing that gown today?"

I thought about that for a few seconds, "Good idea. What about I wear this to the meeting and change into the gown when we convene at Wynyard Street? It'll only take a few seconds to change."

"Okay. Look at this," Seamus opened a document on the laptop. A list of the exiled members of the community, their contact details, date they were exiled, and the reasons for their banishment. All set out in a document. I could've hugged Seamus. Reading my mind, he reached over and enveloped me in a huge bear hug. "Your parents would be so proud. Of everything you've done since you've been back. I'm proud of you. You are honouring your heritage and pushing through your fear."

Rendered temporarily speechless, I jumped up and poured more water into the kettle. I mentally ticked off the list of things I had to do this morning. "Can you send that document to the printer at the office? Print off a dozen copies please. If you don't mind," I added, sliding another coffee towards him.

"Sure. You're coming into the office first, before the meeting?" Seamus clicked the email icon and attached the document to an outgoing email.

"Yes. I'll take my own car, as I want to go past Wynyard Street on the way to the meeting." Spark wound his way around my ankles. I looked down, as his mewing grew louder. Once he knew he had my attention he walked towards the front door. I glanced at Seamus, and we both followed my familiar across the wooden floor. Spark stood at the door, on his hind legs, as if trying to reach the door handle.

I opened the door, my heart pounding, wondering what would be waiting for me on the verandah.

"I didn't expect that," Seamus spoke the words before I could get them of my mouth. I'd been the recipient of a wooden box full of documents and papers before, left on my verandah. I'd received warning notes before, on my car, and via email. Never before had I been the receiver of a pile of old bones. Spark sniffed the skeleton strewn over the welcome mat.

"That's not real, is it?" I kicked the skull with my shoe, pretty sure it was plastic.

"It's not even a good imitation," Seamus agreed. The skeleton pieces were painted a weird grey colour and broken into individual bones. "Not a complete set, though the message is clear I guess."

Spark stood at the top of the steps looking towards the road. I held my finger to my lips and moved over to my kitten. "Hi Spark," I crooned, patting his back. I followed his line of sight and saw a man standing behind a tree, watching my verandah. I didn't recognise him, but the feeling I got was Dean. "Maybe one of his coven members," I told Seamus about him a few minutes as we cleaned up the debris.

"I guess they've underestimated you," Seamus spoke gently, "He held my shoulders gently, and steered me towards the bedroom. "Grab that gown, and whatever else you need for the meeting. Afterwards, let's take a long lunch. Whatever happens."

In a daze, I picked up the gown, checked my reflection in the mirror, and left my bedroom. In the kitchen, I tucked my laptop, phone, wallet and folders into my bag. I caught my best friend watching me, concern etched on his face. "We'll be fine," I said more brightly than I felt.

"I know," he replied. "I need you to know it, to believe it. Your strength and power will grow stronger, with confidence and belief." He touched my cheek, briefly. "You meant what you said last night." His words a statement, not a question.

"Every single word." I saw, as well as felt, the emotion in the air between us. I knew he did too. I wanted to stay there, and not move, not break the moment.

My kitten jumped on his hind legs, patting my knee. I bent and scooped him up. "I know," I whispered, "I'll be fine, and we'll be home later today. It'll be okay." *It'll be okay,* my words echoed in my head.

It really will. The voice was mine, and also my parents, and my grand-mothers, all merged into one.

Chapter Forty-One

I left Seamus at the council office. He, Mikayla and the other councillors were going to join me at the school hall, before 9am. Armed with everything I thought I'd need, I drove to the site in Wynyard Street.

Frank had done an amazing job, the site was cleared of most of the debris. In my mind I pictured the site the way it could be, bigger and better than before. *Don't overthink it, Beth.* Elemental magic was about intuition and gut, not brain and thinking. Being one with the elements. I stood, letting the emotions and energies of the history of the site blend with my magic. My hands wove back and forth, back and forth, a single silver strand of thread visible only to me.

Slowly, slowly, shimmer and shiny...

I let the thread hover there, in the cool early morning air, protected by my grandmother...

"Mr Wellham, the principal, organised a morning breakfast in the park for the children. Our weekly assembly will be held after lunch, that way, you'll have uninterrupted access to the hall for the community meeting." Maria Evans, the school office administrator smiled as she showed me to the hall, where black metal and plastic chairs were set out in rows. "No need to move the chairs when you're finished," she added. "If you need anything, I'm in the office." Maria was a little older than me. I remembered her from school. Her short blonde hair was set in a cute bob style. She wore a black skirt, and a white shirt, with green pinstripes.

"Thanks Maria. Where'd you find that shirt? It's nice." I knew I needed to practice my small talk.

Maria beamed. "I made it myself. I sew a lot of my own clothes; I find it therapeutic." Her mobile rang, she waved to me as she answered it, lodging the large double doors open behind her.

The school hall would easily fit two hundred people seated, with more standing room behind the chairs. At the front of the hall, a stage stood, complete with heavy red curtain. Just in front it was a dais. I sat my laptop bag to one side of it, not planning to use notes or the information I'd gathered, unless I needed to.

I heard voices. A few people peered through the open doors. "Come in, find a seat. Help yourself to tea, coffee, or water," I motioned to the left side of the hall, where Maria had set up an urn and a table stacked with cups, and bottles of water. Mikayla, Seamus and the other councillors arrived with the second wave of residents.

I made my way to where Jan and the others from Wynyard Street had quietly moved into the last row of seats. "Can I get anyone a cup of tea, coffee, or maybe water?" I asked, after we'd exchanged hellos.

"That would be lovely, thank you," Jan replied, "If it's not too much trouble. I know you must be busy."

"I'm not too busy to make sure you are all comfortable," I made eye contact with each of them. The general buzz of a room filling up with people, greeting each other, fed my nervous energy.

Ralph stood. "I'll help carry the drinks back."

We walked past groups of friends hugging and chatting. A quick head count told me we already numbered over one hundred. As I requested, the councillors were each talking to a group of people. Seamus, Lily, Izzie, Lexi and Lara were with Agnes and Mike. I recognised many faces, less sure of the names associated with them. I'd no doubt Seamus, or my parents, would've been able to name most of those gathered in the room.

"I know what they drink," Ralph quickly assembled five cups of tea, two black, the others with milk, and one with sugar. He balanced three of them, while I held the other two and we returned to the group.

I felt a hand gently on my back, as Seamus joined us. "Good morning, everyone, I apologise, but I need to drag Beth away now. I'll come and talk to you after the meeting, if you've time."

I let Seamus steer me towards the front of the room, gathering my energy and my thoughts as we walked. "Are you okay?" he asked as we approached the dais.

I inhaled, and exhaled, expelling the air, and my fears. "I think so, I mean, yes I am." I heard the confidence and strength in my voice.

Seamus did too. "You've got this," he said as he peeled away to the right of the stage, standing with the other councillors.

Standing to one side of the dais, I stared out across the room. Without my glasses the figures at the back were a little blurry, yet Dean, Max and Jacob were easy to spot, standing just inside the doorway. The man I'd seen when we found the skeleton stood near them. I swallowed down the lump in my throat. This meeting wasn't about the coven, as they identified themselves, it was about five people who lost their livelihood.

I straightened my back, squared my shoulders and projected my voice, intending it to sound confident, and strong. "Good morning, everyone. Thank you all for coming. If you'd like to find a seat, we can start."

A silence fell on the room, interrupted only by murmurs as people found spare seats, or chose to stand at the back of the room. "The main reason for the meeting, is to brainstorm ideas for supporting the group who lost their businesses when the Wynyard Street shops were attacked." I chose my words carefully. "An idea has been put forward, and I'd like us to end the meeting with a site visit to explain the details. I know some people have questions for me, as mayor. I propose we discuss options for helping the Wynyard Street tenants first, then I'll take questions, before we move to the site of the fire. How does that sound?"

People nodded, some called out that it sounded reasonable, the main thing was no one yelled anything disparaging. "Redeveloping the site will take time, and while it's the best option long term, I'm hoping we can provide short term solutions that means Jan, Brett, Mary, Tanya, and Ralph won't be disadvantaged."

Half a dozen hands flew up. As we'd prepared earlier, Mikayla took the portable microphone to those wanting to speak. Aida Oates, convenor of the Spirit Town markets spoke first. Tanned from working outside in her garden or at the markets, she wore jeans with purple butterflies and an oversized pink shirt. "I'd like to offer each tenant a free space to trade at our weekly markets, for twelve months. I'll promote your sites, help with the setup, provide gazebos, tables, stands, point of sale, cash floats, whatever you need."

"Thank you, Aida, Mikayla will get your details after we hear from everyone, and she'll arrange a meeting to work out the details. At this point I don't expect anyone to decide anything, we are just gathering ideas, and we'll workshop them early next week." Jan held two thumbs up in response.

Toddy and Cliff stood together, owners of the newsagents and chemist respectably. Both were mid-sixties, maybe older, and although they looked like a strong wind would knock them over, they still turned up and worked all day. Most days. Toddy, the taller of the two spoke. "Cliff and I have been talking. We're getting older, and while we have wonderful staff who can manage our shops without us, we'd like to offer any of the tenants who want a stint at working at either of our stores, a few hours a week, paid work." Cliff nodded encouragingly as Toddy got the words out, leaning on the back of the chair in front for support.

"That's a great offer, thanks Toddy, Cliff." My heart soared at the generosity of the community.

A woman I didn't recognise was next. Younger than me, dressed in a fitted black dress, spoke softly. "My name is Gwenda Dodds, my grandmother passed away a few months ago. She used to teach sewing and needlework. It's my job to work out what to do with all her machines and tools. If Mary could use them, I'm willing to donate the whole lot." She turned to the back, "Of course, only if you could use them."

"That's very generous, thank you, Gwenda. Mikayla will get your details." The vibe in the hall was electric. People whispered to each other, the positive buzz and generosity contagious.

One person remained standing. "It's not a washing machine," the older woman said, staring at the microphone that Mikayla held out, "but I'm retiring from my ironing business to travel. Tanya, you can have all my gear, for free if you want them, irons, ironing boards, steaming tools etc." I recognised Mavis, a long-time friend of my mother.

Before I had a chance to thank her, a male voice called from the side of the room. "What about you Beth? Do you get money from insurance? What are you going to do with the money? Are you helping the tenants in any way?" Most heads in the room turned towards the person who spoke. Max's voice was easily recognised by most of those gathered.

I faced Max but made sure I included the entire auditorium as I spoke. "Every cent of insurance I receive will be put back into the site. I'll make the documentation available to anyone who wants it." In my black shoes, I scrunched my toes, forcing my energy not to escape and hit Max right in the middle of his forehead.

"How do you balance your position of mayor, with your position on the magic council?" This time Dean spoke, the distinct sneer in his voice unmistakable.

"I'm not the only person on either council. The town councillors work as a team, as do the members of the magic council. No one person makes all the decisions. I'm pleased you brought this up, as both councils have been discussing options for inviting any of the residents who've been exiled, the opportunity to return, to live peacefully in Spirit Town. It's been confirmed that over a one-hundred-year period, only five people have ever been sent away from our town. We'll be contacting them, or their descendants, and beginning the discussion." I softened my voice a little, facing away from Dean, "Everyone will be given the opportunity to raise any concerns, and provide feedback."

Seamus moved to stand near me. I moved a little to one side, knowing he wanted to speak. "Let's give Beth's voice a rest," he said. "Most of you know me, I've been around forever."

A wave of laughter rippled through the gathering.

"This is an exciting time for Spirit Town. We've got new farming ideas, an agricultural school with a point of difference, and other initiatives...not all led by our mayor. It's very much a collaborative effort. In the spirit of community input we will be inviting interested parties to attend workshops. So, if a particular initiative interest or concerns you, make a time to speak to us, join with us to make a difference in our town. Stay tuned to our radio, newspaper and social media for information, or contact Mikayla."

A dozen hands shot up. I didn't hear any of the next few minutes' discussion, as a movie reel ran in front of me, depicting a group of ghostly figures ransacking the site of the fire. Dean and Max stared straight at me, grinning. My toes cramped, my stomach too, I pulled my gaze away from them, focusing on the thread I'd left at the site, picturing it protecting the area. I felt every jolt, as the thread worked as an electric fence. Each attempt by the vandals became thwarted by an actual bolt of electricity. Seamus could sense something was wrong. I heard him wrap up the conversation. "Thank you, and if you haven't given Mikayla your name, but you'd like to be involved, contact her, or anyone of us." He glanced at his watch. "While we must wrap this up now, there'll be plenty of other opportunities to work through this together. Thank you all for coming, and for anyone who wants to join us,

we'll be moving to the site at Wynyard Street, to show you the plans for
the site redevelopment."

Chapter Forty-Two

Seamus drove me to the site. I sat in the back of my car, and wriggled the gown on, taking care not to rip any of the delicate fabric. We drove in silence, our minds in unison, as I prepared for the showdown. Discussion and de-brief could happen later.

My heart thumped in my chest. I felt every pulse of blood, as it pumped around my body. At least fifty people were already waiting, with more cars pulling in along the road as we drew into the driveway of the scout hall. The crowd parted as I walked slowly, deliberately to the point in the middle of the site. With each step, and breath, I called on my ancestors, to add to my powers. I sensed my magic growing within and around me. Could anyone else see the elements I sensed? Every particle in the air alive and waiting for me to call upon it.

Glancing around I saw a sea of colours, rather than faces. The auras of the people who gathered were mostly bright, or pastel shades. Auras of the group to one side were sticky and dark. I detached my magic from them, as they tried their best to weigh me down. I didn't need to see their faces to know it was Dean and his coven.

In my mind I saw the map of the site, as clearly as if it rested in front of me, completed and open for business. My voice sounded out loud and strong, as with my hands I created – show and tell. "The new complex will include a green space, complete with trees and flowering plants, a children's play area, park benches and a barbeque." Out of the dirt and concrete rubble trees, plants, and grass started to grow. The thread I'd started earlier in the day bent to my will. A soft surface, safe for children, swings, and a children's play structure emerged from the ground. Wooden seats and a barbeque took shape. "Around two of the sides, will be businesses. In addition to the five shops that used to stand on site, will be a couple of new stores." My body moved in the direction of each piece I wove with my hands. The energy grew stronger, as out of nothing, bricks and mortar created the shell of a long L shaped suite of shops on two sides of the green space growing in the middle of the plot. My energy glowed, as the elements moulded to my bidding.

I managed to ignore the temptation to look at the crowd. The pull of the magic between my fingers was intoxicating. Knowing part of my point was to leave the interior for contractors, to give the project to locals, I slowed my breathing and the weaving of the story. "This is the shell of the new stores. The fit out inside is a project for others." I let my hands fall to my side. "As Beth Harriott, not as mayor, I'll be funding the project. We'll need local workmen to complete the exterior as well as the interior, others to sign off on the construction, electricity, etc."

A couple of painful seconds of silence followed as I faced the crowd. A murmuring started as people whispered to those near them. As the crowd erupted into a round of applause, I realised I'd been holding my breath. Amongst the crowd my eyes caught the smiling faces of Jan, Brett, Ralph, Tanya, Mary, Seamus and the others from the council. Izzie and Lexi were chatting with some of the older members of the congregation. Lara and Agnes stood to one side deep in conversation. Jon and Fred were at the rear, not far from Dean and Max. My nemesis's auras were dull, as if they'd been reprimanded for bad behaviour, their frowns visible from my position. A black van pulled up behind them. With Jacob and two other men, they climbed in the back of the van, slamming the sliding door shut as it sped away. The clapping grew in intensity. "Good riddance," someone yelled from the crowd.

Agnes and Seamus joined me, flanking either side, as I wobbled a little. Magic used more energy than I thought possible, though I felt energised, not drained, but a little light-headed. Agnes lay her hand on my arm. "Thank you, Beth, for your generosity, strength and bravery. Your parents and grandmother spoke of your quiet determination. We've seen that clearly demonstrated today. The whole town community thanks you." She gave Seamus a sideways glance. "That young man next to you looks absolutely famished. I think it's time you took him to lunch." A ripple of laughter ran through the crowd.

"Thank you, Agnes," Seamus said solemnly, the twinkle in his eyes giving him away. "Please, anyone with questions contact one of us at the council and we'll answer as soon as possible. One of us will be in contact with everyone who offered support earlier and meeting invites will go out too."

The gathering dispersed rapidly. The vibe I got was one of positivity. "Will my demonstration of magic have any negative repercussions?" I asked Agnes, as she reached for and held my hand. Seamus's hand found mine too. I sensed their energy seeking and balancing my own. A gentle squeeze from both told me I'd guessed correctly. The energy buzz was like nothing I'd felt, ever.

"Not sure about Dean's next step, but in terms of our town, people may decide to use their magic more openly. We'll deal with that as it happens." Agnes replied. "There's no problem with the use of magic per se, it's about how it's used, and why." Jon nodded in agreement, as he and Fred joined us. Izzie, Lara, and Lexi added to our group.

Jan and the other tenants wandered up from the where they'd been perusing the newly constructed building. "This is amazing." Jan as spokesperson, her voice softer than normal, with tears welling in her eyes. "We don't know how to express our gratitude, except to say thank you, for everything you've done for us."

"People are so generous," Mary murmured softly. "A few people came up to me, offering items I can use."

"I've had the same experience," Tanya agreed. "So many people have asked for me to do their weekly ironing."

Ralph cleared his throat, "The men's shed have had offers of materials, and tools, so thank you," he added gruffly.

"Toddy and Cliff offered us shifts too, and a couple of other businesses said they'd be in touch." Jan added. "It means none of us will have trouble paying our bills."

Letting go of the others, I wrapped my arms around Jan. "I'm so happy for you, all of you. You'll hear from us in the next few days as we work out the details." Mary and Tanya joined in the group hug. Brett and Ralph faces looked like they wished to join us but didn't. Instead, they both shook my hand.

"I hate to break up the party," Seamus smiled at everyone, "But can we reconvene at Evie's? I'm starving, and Beth should eat something, we've got a whole day's worth of work to catch up on."

Chapter Forty-Three

The sign on the door said that the café was closed for a private function for two hours. I raised my eyebrow, as Seamus pushed open the door. Another round of applause greeted me as I followed him. "Three cheers for Beth," Izzie called out. Choruses of *hip hip hooray* bought tears to my eyes.

Evie came forward to greet us. Hugging me she whispered, "thank you."

I opened my voice, but no words came out.

"Beth speechless? The first time in all the years I've known you. You always have something to say," Seamus laughed, ducking as I pretended to whack his arm.

Leading me to a spare seat in between Lara and Lexi, Evie said, "No need to speak. Bessie, Bert and I put together some of your favourite foods, or Seamus's, I'm guessing you like the same foods," she gave a sideways glance to Seamus, "There'll be time for talking later."

As I managed to squeeze out the words, "Thank you," my gaze swept around the table. Someone had reconfigured the tables and chairs into one long table setting that sat twenty people. Fairies must have helped because so much of the fixings normally in place had been moved, but somehow didn't look odd or out of place.

My bestie sat opposite me, between Glen and Jon. My friends, those who worked on council with me, and the Wynyard Street tenants, seated together around the table. In front of me, a veritable feast that included garlic bread, burgers, pizza pieces, hot chips, and bowls of salad sat waiting for me to choose. Pitchers of ginger beer, and mugs of coffee completed the feast. I sipped from the large mug of steaming liquid in front of me. I noticed no one else had started eating. "Please, everyone, start lunch. I'm just taking a moment to appreciate the best mocha in the world."

I wanted to savour every minute of this impromptu gathering. I picked a piece of each food item, added them to my plate, and nibbled through the pile of deliciousness while the others chatted.

"Lexi and I videoed the whole thing. The meeting and the demonstration of your abilities. We'll put together copy for you to approve before it goes out," Izzie stood to leave first. "This was great, thanks for including me," she patted Seamus on the back, in typical Izzie style.

"I'd better be heading back too. Thanks for the invite," Lexi leant in a pecked Seamus on the cheek.

"See?" Seamus joked to Izzie, "instead of whacking my back." Izzie side eyed him. "on second thoughts, forget I suggested it." Izzie obliged, patting him again, a little more gently this time. It struck me Izzie and Lexi were becoming friends as well as colleagues. They even wore similar clothing. Both in black, Lexi's long flowing skirt and Izzie's black shirt, I smiled, pleased Izzie had taken Lexi under her wing while I had my stint as mayor.

Agnes dragged her chair back, "Thank you, young Quinn, for the invitation." Agnes rarely ate any kind of *fast food,* but she'd made an exception. A few chips and crust from a piece of pizza sat on her plate. "Beth, you're well on your way to prove that a gifted person can sit on both councils in Spirit Town, and do so with grace, elegance and style." Without giving me an opportunity to respond, she marched through the door, disappearing as it closed behind her.

Jamie coughed, "I just wanted to say, we owe you an apology, both of you." He nodded at Seamus and me. "On behalf of us all, we're humbled to work with you both for the rest of our term as councillors. We won't be so quick to judge in future."

I held Jamie's gaze. "Thank you, all of you," I held eye contact with the others on council. "I'm looking forward to working with you on all the initiatives we've identified." I refreshed my glass of ginger beer as my work colleagues left the café.

"We're heading off too. Thanks Beth, Seamus." Jan, Brett, Mary, Tanya, and Ralph each patted my shoulder as they passed me on the way to the door.

Fred, Jon, Lara, Seamus and I remained at the table. "Is there anything else we can get you?" Bert and Bessie began collecting the empty plates and mugs.

"Any chance of another mocha, and some chocolate mud cake?" I asked.

"With ice cream?" Seamus added.

"Coming right up," Bessie beamed, hurrying over to the counter, her arms laden with empty plates. Two fairies trailed behind her allowing her to balance it all without spilling the stray pieces of food that wobbled in between the plates.

Bert, wearing a bright pink, green and orange apron that matched Bessies, piled the glasses into the empty pitchers. Prepared with an empty tray, he stacked the jugs on it and headed through the swinging doors that led to the kitchen. A fairy held the door open with her wand. If she hadn't, he would've likely smashed the glasses on the door. I suppressed a smile, which Lara mistook for a yawn.

"Will you have the chance for a rest this afternoon?" she asked sympathetically. "I don't know much about magic, but being in crowds can be exhausting."

The wall clock informed me it was just after 1pm. "I've a couple of hours work to do. First thing though, I'm changing out of this gown. I can't believe I didn't think to take it off before eating. It's lucky I didn't ruin it." I glanced at my lap, confirming no errant pieces of food had collected there. "I'm thinking an early night tonight. What are your plans?"

Lara blushed. I followed her gaze as she looked at Jon. "We're having a quiet dinner and movie night at home."

"Great idea, we might do the same." I caught Seamus's eye.

A comfortable silence fell over the table. I glanced at my friends, as Bessie returned to the table with our dessert. My energy buzzed with anticipation of what would happen next.

The End

Sarah Lewin

If you want to know more about me or my books, here are some details. Alternatively, please make contact via any of the social media listed below:

Email: sarahlewin@sarahlewin.com.au

You Tube: https://youtube.com/@sarahlewinangelwisdom539

Blog: https://sarahlewin.com

Facebook: https://www.facebook.com/SarahLewinAuthorWitchyMysteryBooks

Instagram: https://www.instagram.com/sarahlewin_author/

Amazon: https://amazon.com/author/sarahlewin

Goodreads: https://www.goodreads.com/author/show/43342156.Sarah_Lewin

Book Bub: https://www.bookbub.com/authors/sarah-lewin

My Witchy Mystery Books:

Witch Wisdom Series:

#1 – *Crone Wisdom*

#2 – *Ancient Wisdom*

#3 – *The Wisdom of the Witches*

There are two free novellas in this series

The Coven

Kai's Story

Spirit Town Cozy Mysteries:

#1 – *Autumn Leaves Are Falling*

#2 – *Secrets Ghosts and Whispers*

#3 – *The Ghosts of Spirit Town*

Misty Vale Town Cozy Mysteries:

#1 – *A Very Crafty Christmas*

<u>I also have a range of children's books available, and some more cozy mysteries due for release in 2025.</u>